ELI'S LAST STAND

Holten lashed out at his assailants, his fists made ineffective by the confined area of the alleyway and the tight press of their bodies. Even so, he managed to connect with one prominent prow of nose, which gave off a satisfying crunch and then a torrent of blood. While still free, he whipped the same closed hand into the side of another half-breed who clung to him.

With a soft moan, the mixed-blood let go and crumpled to the alley floor. Finally, the scout was able to pull his Bowie from its sheath and face his final tormentor. Except someone was coming at him from behind!

Bright lights and explosive pain burst in his head as the broad, flat face of a tomahawk smashed into the back of his skull . . .

FORGE AHEAD IN THE SCOUT SERIES
BY BUCK GENTRY

#10: TRAITOR'S GOLD   (1209, $2.50)

There's a luscious red-head who's looking for someone to lead her through the Black Hills of the Dakotas. And one look at the Scout tells her she's found her man — for whatever job she has in mind!

#11: YAQUI TERROR   (1222, $2.50)

The Scout's rescue of a lovely and willing young lady leads him into the midst of a revolution. Even with battles raging around him, Eli proves to her once again that a hard man is good to find!

#12: YELLOWSTONE KILL   (1254, $2.50)

The Scout is tracking a warband that kidnapped some young and lovely ladies. And there's danger at every bend in the trail as Holten closes in, but the thought of all those women keeps the Scout riding hard!

#13: OGLALA OUTBREAK   (1287, $2.50)

When the Scout's long time friend, an Oglala chief, is murdered, Holten vows to avenge his death. But there's a young squaw who's appreciation for what he's trying to do leads him down an exciting trail of her own!

#14: CATHOUSE CANYON   (1345, $2.50)

Enlisting the aid of his Oglala friends, the Scout plans to blast a band of rampaging outlaws to hell — and hopes to find a little bit of heaven in the arms of his sumptuous companion . . .

#15: TEXAS TEASE   (1392, $2.50)

Aiding the Texas Rangers, with the luscious Louise on one side and the warring Kiowa-Apache on the other, Eli's apt to find himself coming and going at exactly the same time!

Available wherever paperbacks are sold, or order direct from the Publisher. Send cover price plus 50¢ per copy for mailing and handling to Zebra Books, 475 Park Avenue South, New York, N.Y. 10016. DO NOT SEND CASH.

#16

THE SCOUT

VIRGIN OUTPOST
BY BUCK GENTRY

ZEBRA BOOKS
KENSINGTON PUBLISHING CORP.

Special Acknowledgments to Mark K. Roberts.

ZEBRA BOOKS

are published by

Kensington Publishing Corp.
475 Park Avenue South
New York, N.Y. 10016

First printing: September 1984

Printed in the United States of America

This book was written in *good taste* for Ormley Gumfudgen, and in praise of the marvelous products of all the International Chili Cookoffs.

B. G.

"Among the best of our scouts have been the half-breeds. They combine the knowledge of the terrain and wildlife of the redman with an understanding of the hostiles' nature and tactics. We can likewise appeal to their white sides in matters of discipline and loyalty. It is regrettable that among these mixed-bloods there are some who are slothful and intemperate. Their excesses oft times lead to betrayal. . . .

—Attributed to a departmental dispatch by General Alfred H. Terry.

Chapter One

Meadowlarks warbled their sweet music across the rills and ravines that scarred the flat, yellow-brown prairie. Here and there, square patches of from twenty to eighty acres showed black where the sod had been turned by steel-bladed plows to reveal the rich gumbo soil beneath. Other straight-edged rectangles showed dark green from the thickly sewn stalks of spring wheat that thrust upward toward the sun in their annual transition from sprouted seeds to tall verdant shoots to rich golden heads of waving grain. Here and there, across the sweeping plain, the low, roughly regular shapes of homesteaders' soddies and the sentinel wooden towers of their windmills broke the symmetry of the variegated patchwork of nature.

At one particularly large soddy—complete with a two-story barn of freshly sawed pine boards—farm wagons, buggies, and saddle horses clustered thickly in the farmyard. It could have been a barn raising—the structure so new it hadn't yet received a coat of paint—or a festive wedding feast, or a christening party. Though a trestle table made of sawhorses and virgin planks groaned under a plethora of food, as was the case on joyful occasions, other, grimmer business had brought these folks together.

To the casual observer, the men approaching the soddy could have been late arrivals. They wore a variety of trousers, coats, hats, and boots. Their manner, though, spoke of something more sinister than tardiness. Voices raised in a hymn reached the ears of the quiet callers.

"Ear-ly in the mor-ning, while the world is slee-ping, We shall came re-joi-cing, bring-ing in the sheaves."

A cold smile lit the face of the leader of these silent visitors who moved stealthily along the outer perimeter of the soddy's fields, where tall green shoots of wheat waved in the breeze and ground lay open to receive the kernels of seed corn. Charlie Roundtree thought the hymn appropriate. They had sung it a lot at the Indian School at Shawnee Mission, Kansas. He had been sent there from his southeast Texas home by way of Indian Territory.

His mother, Jessica Adams before she'd married his father, had insisted on it. It would, she believed, give him a better start. Some start, he mused. His mother should see him now. It would pucker her pussy, he reckoned. If his father hadn't already reamed it out to barn-door size. Charlie motioned his troops forward with a sharp jerk of his hand. Quickly and quietly they moved in toward the sod-block structure that reared up defiantly from the prairie.

"We shall come re-joi-cing, bring-ing . . . in . . . the . . . sheaves."

"Praise the Lord!" Josiah Clamper called out over the heads of his assembled neighbors and friends. His graying brown hair stood up in tufts from his scalp, and the work and weather creases that seamed his reddened face lent it a certain staunchness of character.

"Thank you all for coming. You know why I called this meeting. We've got problems, friends. An' jes' takin' 'em to the Lord ain't gonna get those problems solved. The Lord helps them what helps themselves. So. *We've* gotta do something about it."

"That's the Army's job, Josiah," Hiram Baxter stated, a note of belligerence in his rusty voice.

The sounds of their discussion drifted clearly to Charlie Roundtree on the late afternoon breeze. Their words amused him.

"The Army's not doin' anythin', Hiram," Clamper responded. "Since this outbreak of attacks on our farms began, that damned do-nothing, Waterstratt hasn't moved his hind end to do a thing for us. He says that since the witnesses saw men in white folk's clothing, it's a job for the Ford County sheriff. Well, we done talked to Bat

11

Masterson. He says the sign indicates it's Injuns."

"Well, whoever done it," another homesteader growled, "I say it's the Army's doin' to stop it. Ain't they out here to protect us?"

"Yes. From hostile action by Injuns. An' the high and mighty Colonel Lemuel Waterstratt don't put no stock in what Masterson says. Oh, he's sent out patrols, all right. But they's clear the hell an' gone out on the Colorado border, lookin' for Arapahoes an' Cheyenne. There ain't no Arapahoes or Cheyenne wearin' white man's clothes."

"Waterstratt knows that," Hiram shot back. "I think he's only tryin' to do something to make it look like the boys in blue is earnin' their keep. The war was over a long time ago. We don't need soldiers. We need more lawmen and a decent program to help support farmers."

"The government don't care, Hiram," Hal Akers joined in. "They've got their nice, comfy jobs back there in Washington, big pay in cash money and all of that. Why, from that distance us farmers don't look no bigger'n a speck of dust. Josiah's right. If we want somethin' done, we gotta do it ourselves."

"Like what?" a farm wife demanded.

Outside, Charlie Roundtree made a quick disposition of his men. He sent them to three sides of the farmstead, so that enfilading fire could cut down the greatest number in the least time. Satisfied, he settled down to wait.

"We got to send a delegation to Fort Dodge. Make Waterstratt understand the danger we're in. We oughta set out someone to watch the countryside, give us early warning."

"Not me, I got crops to tend." "Me, too." "Too much work around my place for that sort of gallyvantin'." The voices rose in protest.

"We could use little bitty boys. Ten years or younger. They ain't gonna do any fightin'—only look around and report back what they see," Akers pressed. "If'n we don't do somethin', whoever's responsible for this is gonna level every farm an' ranch from here to Pratt and Great Bend. I got a stake here an' I don't intend to lose it. I proved up my claim back in 'sixty-nine an' I'm gettin' more acres under cultivation each year. You boys know how it is. We're all in the same boat. Give us two good years an' our wimmen folks will be able to see cash money in their pocketbooks. Are we gonna let a bunch of hoodlums, redskins or white, spoil that for us?"

"No!" A shouted chorus rose.

"Then let's decide. Uh . . . I'm sorry for runnin' off so much, Josiah. This here is your meetin'."

"Couldn't have said it better myself, Hal. Well, boys, the ladies have got us some mighty nice vittles out there. Fried chicken, tater salad, beets, and the like. Be a shame to let it go to waste. Let's round this thing up an' get to the eatin'. I'd like to call for some volunteers to go with me to Fort Dodge. Who'll do it? Won't take more'n two days."

"I'll go," Nathaniel Speers offered.

"Count me in, Josiah," Luther Miller added.

Two more tendered their services. Satisfied, Josiah turned to Hal Akers. "I'd be beholdin' if you sort of set up a schedule for protectin' our places, Hal. An' you might look into that rovin' patrol idea. With no school for more'n thirty miles, it might just take some of the vinegar outta our boys. My Jimmy will be one of them." Josiah clapped his ham hands together in lieu of a gavel. "That's about it, folks. Now let's eat."

As the meeting broke up, talk turned to the best ways of setting up defenses and of barricading homes against attack. The men and women began to stream out into the yard. Young boys joined them from inside the barn, shrill voices whooping with excitement and good appetite. Out of the kitchen portion of the soddy, girls came with hot, fresh-baked bread, pitchers of spring-cooled milk, and a small hogshead of homemade beer.

Charlie Roundtree crouched with a third of his force behind the far siderails of the pole corral attached to the long side of the barn. Before he and his raiders could be spotted, Charlie rose to full height, brought one arm up above his head, and then dropped it in a signal.

Immediately, clear, staccato notes belled from a bugle as it played the cavalry charge. The marauders came from their hiding places, rifles at their shoulders.

"Take aim. . . . Fire!" Charlie commanded in a stentorian voice. "Load . . . take aim . . . fire!"

Two disciplined volleys crashed out. Men and women fell at every point in the farmyard. Children screamed and cried. Several farmers rushed toward their wagons, where they had left their rifles and shotguns—only to discover them in the hands of grinning, dark-faced men with hawk noses and black eyes . . . all dressed in white men's clothing.

"Load . . . take aim . . . fire!" Charlie bellowed again.

Bullets splintered wooden doors and frames, shattered a kerosene lantern, and ripped puffs of brown dust from the soddy walls. Two more of the homesteaders toppled to the ground.

Tommy, the oldest Clamper boy—thirteen—darted toward where his mother stood in frozen terror, arms clutching a large crockery platter of bread loaves. But suddenly the lad seemed to take flight. Lifted off his feet by a huge four-hundred-five-grain lead slug, Tommy sailed through the air, a gout of blood erupting from his chest as the offending bullet ripped apart his sternum. He fell at his mother's feet, his lifeless eyes staring up at eternity from a pale face, his head twisted at an odd, unnatural angle.

"Tommy!" Nellie Clamper shrieked. "Oh, God, Tommy!"

Screams from the suddenly bereaved mother broke the paralyzing shock of the surprise attack. The hardened plainsmen fell back to the soddy in disarray, dragging their dead and wounded in after them. Some, who had kept their weapons at their sides during the meeting, returned fire, covering the noncombatants and ducking last through the doorway.

Once inside, the men, and some women, took stations at windows and gunloops in the two doors, and the volume of their fire increased.

15

Women and children wailed in agony and horror, and gunshots deafened everyone in the confined space.

"Who are they?" Hal Akers asked as he drew a bead on one raider who had climbed the poles of the corral.

"Damned if I know," Hiram Baxter replied. "But there's sure a hell of a lot of them."

"They . . . killed . . . my . . . boy." Josiah Clamper sobbed as he levered another round into his Spencer rifle.

"Look!" a farmer at a window closer to the barnyard shouted. "They're goin' to run off the stock. All your cows, Josiah. An' all our horses. Damn them! Damn the rotten bastards an' damn the Army for not helping us."

With wild whoops and war cries, Charlie Roundtree's ragtag army of renegades and half-breeds swarmed over the farmstead. Two of them ignited coal-oil saturated rags and heaved them onto the roof of the soddy. Another pair fired the barn with sulphurous lucifer matches. In a dusty swirl, the attackers finished rounding up the stock and began to drive it away. A dozen dropped to their knees, faced back toward the soddy, and fired a final, controlled volley.

Then they, too, leaped to their feet and ran off hooting and hollering in the best Indian style.

The marauders left behind flaming buildings and shattered and demoralized homesteaders.

A mutter of voices came from the early patrons

along the bar in the Long Branch. Most of these citizens of Dodge City had dropped in for a routine, daily drink on the way home from work. The town was booming. The previous year the railroad had arrived and with it had come the trail herds.

Suddenly, saloons, dance halls, and eating establishments began to spring up on every available piece of bare ground. Often little more than two-by-four frames with tent canvas thrown over them, some structures in the central part of town had taken on a look of permanence. Premier among these "solid" businesses were Mayor Jim "Mad Dog" Kelly's Dodge House, George Hoover's mercantile, and the Long Branch Saloon. The cattle pens, railroad yard, feed and grain barn, and other enterprises employed a large number of people.

The local men who considered themselves "regulars" preferred the more civilized amenities of the Gentlemen's Bar in the Dodge House or the Long Branch to the wild and woolly stews frequented by the drovers during the long season from May to September. Those regulars now strung along the splendid, highly polished mahogany bar of the Long Branch talked of cattle prices, the expected arrival of the first herd, and of the local events and politics of Dodge City. Not so the five men seated around a large, circular deal table with a green baize covering.

They had been there since nearly noon. A tall, ruggedly handsome man stood out from the other players, though their number included such

17

luminaries as Chalk Beeson, George M. Hoover, and Ed Masterson, off-duty city marshal. The stranger wore a buckskin shirt, not in itself unusual for Dodge City, though the narrow trim of beadwork was in the design of the Sioux. He had a far-seeing demeanor, highlighted by the cool, steady gray eyes, set comfortably apart in his wide, lean face, which was made distinctive by an aquiline nose and thin, mobile lips that made one feel they were equally at home with a smile as with a grimace of purposeful strength. The long fingers of his wide hands had been browned by sun and weather, as had the flesh of his cheeks and brow. He moved his hands with the grace of a professional gambler or an accomplished gunhawk. At a glance, he seemed to have nothing in common with the man to his left.

Of moderate stature, Clive Newton could boast of little beyond a paunch so well-developed that his vest did not cover a wide band of shirt between it and his trousers. He wore a slightly shiny suit that spoke of better times, and a large diamond glittered on the stickpin of his florid necktie. The gold of his gaudy ornament, if indeed it was such, had tarnished to a brassy green. His watery blue-green eyes moved with nervous jerks and his small, mean mouth spoke of a withered soul. That he was a card sharp, down on his luck, no one had any doubts. His play during the afternoon had been skillful, though tainted by a hint of desperation. Now he attempted to maintain a bland, non-committal expression like those of the men who faced him.

"It's up to you, Eli," Ed Masterson reminded the buckskin-clad player opposite him.

Eli Holten, chief scout for the Twelfth United States Cavalry, smiled. "Sorry, Ed. I was thinking about Della Caldwell."

"No doubt," Masterson returned dryly.

"Not like that. I was wondering how her business is faring way off in Denver."

"Excellently, likely as not."

"I know it is if she kept that pretty little thing ye brought in here for her, Eli," Mad Dog Kelly put in. "That one was a real moneymaker. Sure an' she screwed the be-Jazus outta every man jack she got her hands on."

"Are we here to gossip or play poker?" Clive Newton snapped.

"Sorry, Clive. It's up to me, huh?" Eli Holten inquired in a gentle tone.

"Right. Right. Get on with it or fold."

"I'll see your raise, Ed, and . . ." Eli dragged his move out as he took another peek at his cards. He wanted to put up everything he owned—his horse, saddle, guns, and money. He had the winning hand, of that he was sure. Hell, he held the highest hand of the entire afternoon. The thought of one quick, big killing inflamed his blood. Not ordinarily a betting man, Eli found he had a sudden urge to plunge.

Then reason and common sense prevailed. He still had to get back to Fort Rawlins. Dakota Territory was a long way away. A modest sum of money sat before him, the product of slow, though steady winning. He quickly added it. Forty-three dollars. Eli dug into the pocket of his whipcord trousers for seven more.

"I'll raise you fifty dollars."

The gold and silver coins made a musical tinkling as they fell among the chips, folding money, and other hard cash.

"Fifty!" Clive exclaimed. "You must be mighty proud of that hand. But . . . I'll see you . . . just to keep you honest."

It took every last cent the down-and-out gambler had. He had been compelled to dig into a small leather poke to find enough. To his left, Chalk Beeson closed up his pasteboards and tossed them into the center.

"I'll see your raise and . . . call," Ed Masterson declared, an amused smile on his face that revealed nothing.

Beside him, George Hoover had already folded.

"Well then," Eli announced with warm gratitude as he slapped down his cards. "Looks like the best hand has it. Aces over kings, full. Thank you for the donations, gentlemen."

"Not so fast," Clive Newton said nastily. "This was a round for good hands, it seems," he went on, nervousness at last betraying him. "I've got nines . . . four of them." With a confident sneer he reached for the pot.

"Sorry, fellers," Ed Masterson announced through a sweet, benevolent smile. "Read these and weep. The big one."

A handful of red decorated the green table. Hearts. From the ace to the ten. "First damned royal flush I've seen in two years. Mighty nice for me that *I* had it."

Clive Newton jerked back his fingers as though burned. He gawked at the supreme hand and stifled a scream of mortal agony. Three hands like that in a single turn? And the other players had to be holding something to have stayed through two raises. It couldn't be. Years of card sense and mastery of every slick trick in the game, from marking and shaving to dealing seconds, shouted at Clive that no matter the odds, no matter the fall of the duckets, this simply couldn't be happening. He groaned softly and his hands trembled as he sat back and wiped a fresh discharge of cold, oily sweat from his brow. No. This just couldn't be happening.

Eli experienced a horrible sinking feeling in his gut. Good thing he had held back something. Despite his disappointment, though, he couldn't help but feel an overwhelming sense of admiration for the charming, yet cool and poker-faced city lawman, Ed Masterson.

"You sucked me in good, Ed. Well done. Winner buys a round?" Eli asked as he stretched out his right arm to shake hands with the winner.

"Sure thing."

"Damn you all!" Clive Newton shrieked in a strangled voice.

The next instant, he kicked back his chair, making a loud screeching noise, and rose so rapidly the piece of oak furniture loudly toppled over. A small, brass furniture-fitted pepperbox appeared in his left hand. The .31-caliber, five-shot Manhattan pointed alternately at Ed Master-

21

son and the scout.

"You're in it together. I know you are," the distraught gambler raved. "You cheated. The game was fixed. You," he declared, as he indicated Eli Holten with the muzzle of the wicked little hide-out gun, "and Beeson here, and Masterson. Thought you could take me easy, didn't you? Well, you won't get away with that. I'm taking that money you crooked outta me, and yours to boot, and I'm getting out of here."

Eli's gun hand remained stretched out across the table. With his left, he pulled his Bowie knife, and with an arcing, backhand swing, he slashed the underside of Newton's gun arm. Fiery pain brought a flash of pale white to blanch the gambler's face and his suddenly colorless lips formed a startled oh.

Before Newton could react, before he had even released his grip on the deadly .31 pepperbox, Holten reversed his strike with the finely honed blade and buried it to the hilt in the treacherous gambler's solar plexus. From across the table, a silver and black blur streaked past his face.

Reflex action had begun to tighten the trigger of the Manhattan pepperbox, its muzzle only inches from the scout's middle, when Ed Masterson lashed out with his cane. The heavy cast-silver head struck Clive Newton's arm and batted the weapon upward. The .31 spat nastily and discharged a bullet into the ceiling. Then Clive Newton's madly glittering blue-green eyes rolled upward in his head and he fell away, pulling the Bowie free of his body in the process.

"Damn, that one was close," Eli said, tight-lipped.

"Don't drip blood on the table," Ed Masterson remarked, nodding toward the Bowie that Eli still clutched. "Chalk won't take kindly to that."

"You bet I won't," Beeson growled in mock anger. A white tension line still circled his mouth.

Eli bent to wipe his blade clean on the dead gambler's suit coat. As he did, the batwings flew wide and a large, dark silhouette blotted out the wedge of sunset-tinged blue sky beyond.

Dressed as usual in high, stove-pipe boots, black trousers, vest and coat, with a white shirt and a narrow, ebon string tie, Wyatt Earp paused a moment, ever-ready six-gun dangling from his right fist. Slowly, without comment, he surveyed the scene. Then, with long, purposeful strides he crossed the room.

In the silence each strike of Earp's bootheels resounded loudly in the high-ceilinged, plushly decorated barroom of the Long Branch. Wyatt stopped at the table and glowered at the standing men.

A tense moment passed, then the deputy city marshal tipped back his black, flat-crowned hat and worked his generous lips into a semblance of a smile.

"Damn, Ed. Let you have a day off and you get into trouble. What was it this time?"

Masterson advanced slightly toward his deputy and rested his weight on the cane. "That feller on the floor, Wyatt, said his name was Clive Newton. He lost his entire stake to me on the last hand. You can tell he's a down-and-out cardslick. Somethin' snapped and he went wild. Pulled a gun. If it hadn't been for Eli here, he'd have done me for sure."

"Ed had something to do with that, Wyatt. He knocked Newton's gun hand away before the feller poked a little hole in my middle."

"That's right, Wyatt," Chalk Beeson put in. "Holten was stretched across the table to shake Ed's hand. Both of 'em was caught cold when this Newton drew on 'em."

Earp glanced from one man to the next and lastly at the body, sizing up the situation. Then he nodded to Jim Kelly. "With the mayor and two of the town's leading citizens as witnesses, I suppose I'll have to accept that it was self-defense."

"Remember whose deputy you are," Ed Masterson growled, slightly irritated at the air of superiority Earp had assumed.

"Not for long, Ed," Wyatt returned with a smile. "I've been offered a place with Bat at the Ford County Sheriff's Office. Also a post as deputy U.S. marshal for Western Kansas. That's what I was on my way over here to tell you when I heard the shot."

"Well," Ed Masterson said warmly. "Congratulations, Wyatt. Which one are you going to take?"

"I don't know that yet. Anyway, I'd sort of like to buy you all a drink. Let's step up to the bar. Howie," Wyatt called to the saloon swamper. "Go get Doc Weems. Tell him he's got another stiff in here."

"Yessir, Mister Earp," the balding, perpetually

nervous handyman stammered.

"You know, Ed, the way you handled that cane, it oughtta been you they called Bat instead of your brother, Will," Chalk Beeson declared as the five men stepped up to the rail and reached for glasses.

Light laughter followed the remark, though Eli Holten could only feel relief.

Chapter Two

Doc Weems held the coroner's inquest right there at the bar some twenty minutes later. The corpse of Clive Newton, covered with a gaily painted strip of canvas left behind by a theatrical troupe, remained where it had fallen.

"Seems simple enough," Weems concluded, after listening to the testimony of the witnesses. "Death by misadventure. Poor dumb feller picked the wrong place and time, in front of the wrong people, to lose control of himself. I'll sign the death certificate accordingly, Marshal Masterson. This hearing is adjourned. Gimme a drink."

Two mortuary assistants removed the body as the crowd began to break up. After a few words of encouragment and an equal number of drinks, Eli Holten found himself alone at the bar.

"A fine state of affairs," the scout thought silently to himself. "Alone, broke, another eight hundred miles between Dodge City and Fort Rawlins. Great idea. Come to Dodge, visit old friends—and get cleaned out by one." Hell, his dark ramblings went on, he hadn't even money to rent a room. A sudden revelation struck him.

"Sampson, let me have another beer," the scout called as he inched a quarter out of his pocket. His papers from General Corrington at Fort Rawlins were as good as a letter of credit. They would at least get him three hots and a cot at the nearby army post, Fort Dodge. He could even, if he worked it right, draw an advance on his salary. Not all had been lost after all.

"You look in need of company, Eli," said the throaty, seductive voice of Beatrice Reid.

The curvaceous, auburn-haired beauty had come on duty only minutes before and no one had yet told her of the afternoon's activities. She offered a broad, generous smile as she sidled up beside the scout. Her breasts, though not over-large, temptingly swelled the bodice of her low-cut costume. Feathers and frills decorated the scanty sea-green outfit and net stockings of the same color highlighted her long, well-shaped legs. Only the slightest tinge of cosmetics, artfully applied, emphasized the classic beauty of her face. Her creamy complexion extended all the way to the tips of her slender fingers, where nature provided ample shading and no polish had been employed.

"I'm afraid I'd be rather poor company, Bea," Eli told her.

"Why's that, handsome?" the exquisite soiled dove cooed. Her smile revealed small, even white teeth.

"First off, Ed Masterson cleaned me out at poker. Then some down-on-his-luck gambler tried to gun us both down and forced me to kill him."

Bea's startingly emerald eyes widened with shocked surprise. "Oh, my. Rather a bad afternoon."

"More so than you think. It's too late to start out now, but once I get to Fort Dodge, I have a place to stay until I can draw against my pay. Until then I'm poorer than church mice." Eli looked down at two dimes, change given him by Sampson.

For a moment, Bea's eyes took on a faraway cast, her face taut with contemplation. "Well, if you have no objection to staying up late, I think something can be done about that."

"How do you mean?"

"I get off when the Long Branch closes, at two. You need a place to sleep. I'm offering my bed. Simple as that."

"I, ah, don't want to impose, Bea," the scout offered weakly. "Especially when I haven't even the price of a Delmonico's Blue Plate Special."

"No imposition . . . and it's free." Bea's sea-green eyes twinkled with anticipation. "I'll . . . not even turn any tricks tonight. Save it all . . . for you."

"I . . . uh . . . hardly know what to say."

"Try thanks, Eli. I know how, uh, ready you always are." Her hand flicked to the scout's crotch and lightly tweaked the impressive bulk of his dormant organ. It remained inactive no longer.

Eli felt it rise and grinned mischievously. The night wouldn't be a total bust after all.

At ten minutes past two in the morning, Beatrice handed Eli the key to her small accommodation above Professor Dodson's Musical Emporium. On the floor below, Dodson sold guitars, fiddles, and harmonicas, along with a respectable volume of sheet music. He also managed occasionally to turn an upright piano. To supplement his income, he gave lessons to all and sundry, and rented out unused portions of his establishment. Eli turned the bolt and twisted the knob. He eased the door open and they entered.

"Here we are," Bea said airily as she lighted a kerosene lamp.

A soft, rosy glow filled the neat, if Spartan quarters. A large rag doll occupied the center of the coverlet on a sturdy iron bed. Strangely enough, it didn't seem out of place. Bea went to a sideboard and opened the glass cabinet. From it she took a cut-glass decanter of a pale amber fluid.

"My secret vice. Fine French brandy. I have it sent up from New Orleans. I like a small glass after work. It lets me relax."

With fluid grace she poured some of the amber liquid into two medium-sized balloon glasses and handed one to the scout. He smiled across the rim, eyes twinkling with the pleasure of discovery. How different a life these girls lead from that

29

which most expect, he mused. They drank and set the stemmed vessels aside.

Without preamble, Bea slid her compact, still youthful body out of her cloudlike finery. In net hose, attached at the tops to the fasteners of a midriff-high corset, her tiny feet still encased in high-heeled shoes, Bea became a classic statue of ancient times. Her alabaster breasts, pink-tipped, with wide thick areolas, presented Holten with an image of delight. Unconsciously, he licked his lips, as though hungry to partake of the rich feast they promised. A growing pressure thickened in his loins.

"Aaah. That's better. I get to feeling as though I'm packed in that like peaches in a can. Take off that shirt, Eli, and get comfortable." She eyed the bulge at his crotch. "Take off . . . everything, hummm?"

Swiftly, the scout complied. Bea had the delightful pleasure of discovering that her hospitality would be rewarded inch by hard inch as Eli showed his appreciation of the surroundings and her seductive body by revealing an ever-expanding housewarming gift that swayed like a storm-tossed sapling as it climbed to its arched fullness.

Bea crouched before him and took his rigid member in both trembling hands.

Slowly, with practiced skill, she began to fondle him. Tremors of pleasure quaked through Eli's body as she squeezed on the out stroke, released on the in. Gradually, her tempo increased, until Eli shivered with sheer delight.

Impulsively, her own body hungry and raging for satisfaction, Bea leaned forward and kissed the huge, purple-red tip. "No. We're not going to waste it like that on a hand job." She rose and led her admirer to the bed.

"This is Sissy," Bea declared as she indicated the doll. "She loves to watch. Sometimes she even wants to get in on the game. If I had a little daughter, I'd like to teach her all about it, too."

Bea lay back on the thick, goose-down coverlet and flung her arms wide in a welcoming gesture. Even more accommodating to Eli's eyes was the thick thatch of auburn hair that surrounded Bea's swollen mound, its dew-damp lips spread wide and coaxing.

Eli joined her, the stout columns of his legs resting between her creamy thighs. Slowly he lowered himself until the burning head of his tumescent phallus nuzzled in the stray strands of deep russet fur that screened her ultimate treasure. With one had, he guided the sensitive nub to the protrusion of her joy bulb and began to massage it with a circular motion.

"Aaaah . . . yessss, Eli. That's it. Ooooh, sooo goood. More. Ah, more and more. Faster. Fas . . . Eiiii! The bells! Don't you hear them? They're ringing. Riiiinging!" Bea thrust herself against him in wild abandon as the first genuine, utterly satisfying climax she had experienced in four years as a soiled dove crashed over her like hurricane-tormented waves. At the peak of her release, Holten entered her, driving to pierce the final veil and plumb her uttermost depths.

Holten lost no time in demonstrating even further how much he enjoyed the warmth of her hearth . . . and further . . . and further . . . until in squeals of joy, Bea burst. With undreamed-of fits of generosity, she ground her body against his until their protruding hip bones bruised each other. The tight, clinging, undulating contractions of her fiery channel seared the flesh of Holten's staff and sent sensations of sheer delirium pulsating through his long, lean frame.

On they plunged, a runaway team in perfect tandem motion.

Deeper Eli drove his massive ember into that glorious chamber.

At last mighty spasms contracted Bea's pulsating canal, milking the vitality of the scout until he detonated.

Surge after surge of sweet nectar escaped from the wildly stimulated beast that ravened within Bea's magnificent stables, washing over her with harmonious paeans of mutual fulfillment.

With a final, lingering series of slow, deep plunges, Eli brought Bea to yet another cataclysmic eruption. Then his glidingly rapturous column of thrilled flesh withdrew, as though reluctant to leave so enchanting a land. The contented couple fell prone across the bed, exhausted from all their conviviality. For the happy length of a hundred heartbeats, the room remained silent.

"Ding-dong. Ding-dong," Eli drawled softly.

"Wha . . . what are you talking about, Eli?"

"The bells. My God, I thought they would crack

they rang so hard."

Bea dissolved into a wild fit of laughter. "Oh . . . oh, oh, my yes. You surely rang them for me."

The next instant, a heavy knock fell on the door.

"Bea? Bea, honey, are you in there?"

"What the hell?" the scout demanded, coming bolt upright in the bed.

"Please, sweetheart. Please listen to me. All is forgiven. I . . . I'm sorry for yelling at you like that. Please . . . please, honey. If you'll just give up that awful job at the Long Branch and come back to me, we can be married. I mean it. Then . . . then my farmhouse will ring with the happiness of our blissful life together."

"Who the hell is that?" Eli demanded in a growl, as one hand reached for his trousers and the other for his holstered Remington.

"Ooh!" Bea cried in vexation. "It . . . it's Billy."

"Billy who?"

"Billy's a farmer. Bill Fieldhouse is his name. He . . . he wants to marry me."

"Oh . . . shit," Holten gulped as he hurried to wriggle into his buckskin shirt.

A sudden change came over Beatrice Reid. There at the door stood a rich beau whom she thought she had lost forever. Although not the handsomest of men, he represented the stability long absent from her life. On the other hand, here beside her struggling to dress, was the first man ever to give her utter satisfaction. A penniless, itinerate, rootless scout for the Army, no less. It was a tough decision.

33

"Hurry!" she hissed. "You've got to get out of here right now."

"But how?"

"Use the window. I don't care. Only . . . only, that's my Billy Fieldhouse and I'm not going to pass up this opportunity again. Go on, Eli. It was fun . . . but—"

"Yeah. Yeah. I know."

Louder knocks sounded on the frail partition. Caught in *flagrante*, so to speak, Eli had no time to pull on his boots, or to fasten the belt of his trousers. The door rattled in its frame and threatened to collapse inward. Angry growls came from beyond it.

"If . . . if'n you got another man in there, I'll trim off his balls and feed 'em to him," Bill Fieldhouse threatened.

Eli drew his Remington.

"Stop that!" Bea hissed at Eli like a snake. "If you so much as char a hair on that fine, loving man's head, I'll tell Ed Masterson that you shot him for the fun of it. There's a back way, once you get on the balcony outside my window. You'd better get, Eli. Or else . . ."

Holten collected the remainder of his belongings and moved unsteadily to the window. There he paused, trying to work his right boot on. In a flash, Bea came to his side and threw up the sash.

"Go on, go on," she demanded breathlessly. Then over her shoulder to the battered door. "In a minute, honey pot. I'm . . . I'm makin' ready for you, sweet toes."

"*Sweet toes?*" Holten mouthed silently to him-

34

self, his tongue gagging over the words.

Quickly he stumbled through the window onto a narrow balcony. The boards creaked threateningly as Holten negotiated the confined passage to his freedom. He heard the door flung open behind him and then delighted squeals as true love had its way and the sweethearts at last embraced, arms entwined in fond reconciliation. How wonderful, he thought. Pure hearts triumph over passion.

It made him want to puke.

"Corporal of the Guard . . ." came the familiar cry from the sentry at the main gate of Fort Dodge.

God! What was he doing dragging himself in here at four in the morning? Broke and chased out of a whore's room, Eli Holten presented an example of ruin and degradation. He halted at the tall, closed portals and waited. With a clatter, the corporal arrived, two additional members of the guard mount in tow. Eli rummaged in an inside pocket of his vest and produced a stained, weatherproofed envelope.

"Who are you, mister, and what are you doing here?" the youthful, blond noncom demanded.

"I'm Eli Holten, chief scout for the Twelfth Cavalry at Fort Rawlins, Dakota Territory."

"Strayed a bit off the trail, didn't ya?" the bleary-eyed NCO said through a snicker.

"Wipe that sneer off your face, Corporal!" Eli's voice cracked like a bullwhip. Suddenly his tiredness and defeat sloughed away and the old fire of his longtime profession returned. "A chief scout ranks with a major, sonny. Don't you damn well forget that, or you'll be back earning thirteen dollars a month. Now open this fucking gate and let me in."

"Uh, y-yes, sir!" the hapless corporal stammered, saluting.

"The one thing this position don't earn me is a salute. You'd best remember that, too, boy," Eli growled as he led his mount through the small sally port cut in the left-hand gate of the main entrance to Fort Dodge. "An' get me someone with rank. Lots of rank."

Sgt. Maj. Wilson Reilly Keogh O'Brannigan did not like being awakened for any reason in the middle of any night. He made that point painfully clear to a trembling Corp. Michael Delehanty as the senior NCO of Fort Dodge rose grumpily from his bunk, took a swig from a close-at-hand bottle of rye whiskey, and belched appreciatively.

"Damn yer bleedin' heart, Delehanty. Why 'tis it that ye've got to be awakenin' me in the middle of this fucking night? Sure an' did ye see some wee leprechauns a-hoofin' it on th' top o' the mess hall is it?"

"N-no, Sergeant Major."

"Then what in the name o' hell brought ye here to disturb a man's sleep in the wee hours o' marnin'?"

"A man at the gate, Sergeant Major. He—"

"A man at the gate 'tis it? An' that's enough to

ruin me vital few hours of slumber, 'tis it? Would ye be likin' a date with the stockade, Car'pril Delehanty?"

"N-n-no, Sergeant Major. Only he—"

"He what, lad? Spit it out, damn yer hide. Ye've done waked me up, I might as well hear the worst o' it." O'Brannigan took another swig from his bottle.

"H-he . . . ah, claims to be chief scout for the Twelfth, Sergeant Major."

"*Claims?*" Has he papers, man?"

"He does that, Sergeant Major."

"An' what does them papers read, Car'pril?"

"That he is the chief scout for the Twelfth United States Cavalry, on detached service to Texas, Sergeant Major. Signed by a general named Corrington, Frank Corrington."

"Ah! Gen'ril now, is it? Ol' Fightin' Frank got hisself a star, did he? Sure an' that's good news. Come now," O'Brannigan went on, his mood lightening. "Show me to this feller an' we'll see if he's all he's cracked up to be."

"Yer Mister Holten, are ye?" Sergeant Major O'Brannigan demanded of the visitor after he had given the papers a meticulous study under the light of a lantern provided by the corporal of the guard.

"I am."

"Sure an' I recognize the handwritin' o' me good old friend, Frank Corrington. But I've no notion

37

of what Chief Scout Eli Holten looks like an' these papers don't tell me. You've some way o' provin' this?"

"I . . ." Holten offered a weak grin. "Frank Corrington likes fine brandy and good cigars. He had a special field case constructed, all padded nice-like so his treasures didn't get broken while on campaign. As I recall, he told me that a troop sergeant he had at the time obtained it for him through contacts the sergeant had developed with the Corps carpenters' shop. That sergeant's name was, I believe, Wilson R. K. O'Brannigan. Would you happen to be familiar with that story?"

"By coincidence, I happen to be the self-same Wilson O'Brannigan, at yer service, Mister Holten," the sergeant major replied, beaming. "Sure an' that's not a story ol' Fightin' Frank would be tellin' to jist anyone. Welcome to Fort Dodge. Please come in an' make yerself at home. We'll be for providin' ye a bunk and oats fer yer mount. Car'pril Delehanty, see to it far Chief Scout Holten, if ye please."

Taken aback by this sudden change, Delehanty nearly stammered again in making his reply. He did direct Eli to the stable, where a sleepy duty soldier made a stall available for Sonny. Then he led the weary scout to an unused dwelling on officers' row. Eli gave him thanks and shut the door behind him. Too tired to light a lamp and lay out his few possessions, he fell, fully dressed, across the narrow army bunk.

Lost to the world, he didn't hear the gruff query

from outside, directed at Sergeant Major O'Brannigan.

"Who is that, Sergeant Major?"

Wet snores ripped the air in the officers' quarters when Sergeant Major O'Brannigan entered twenty minutes later. He crossed to the bunk where a supine Eli Holten lay in deathlike slumber. He reached down and roughly shook the scout's boot. Well aware of the touchy nature of frontiersmen such as scouts and the like, the top soldier of Fort Dodge had no desire to find himself with a Bowie stuck in his gullet, or a fist hammering his face.

"Unnh! Wha . . . aaah!" Eli Holten growled and snarled his way to wakefulness. "Oh . . . ah, it's you, O'Brannigan," the scout said as he rubbed his gritty eyes. "What time is it?"

"Four thirty-nine, Mister Holten. Ah, Colonel Waterstratt's compliments, sir, an' he requests the presence of the chief scout of Fort Rawlins."

"Who is Colonel Waterstratt, by the way?" Eli grumbled, still fighting the effects of deep sleep.

"Lt. Col. Lemuel Waterstratt, commanding officer of Fort Dodge, Mister Holten."

"Can't it wait until after First Call, Sergeant Major?" Eli inquired as he scraped a hand over the thick stubble on his chin.

"Uh . . . beggin' yer pardon, Mister Holten, but the good Colonel said now. Right . . . now."

Chapter Three

Unwashed, unshaven, and semiconscious, Eli Holten stumbled into the office of Lt. Col. Lemuel Waterstratt. To the scout's relief, the commander of Fort Dodge appeared every bit as drowsy and unkempt as his guest. Waterstratt pointed to a chair as he scratched his red flannel-covered pot belly. Bright gold suspenders, trimmed in army blue, held up a regulation pair of dark blue, woollen trousers that had wide yellow stripes over their outside seams. The Lieutenant Colonel's short-cropped black hair managed to look as though it had recently endured a whirlwind, tufts of it pointed up at odd angles as he ran thick, blunt fingers through it in an attempt to command it into formation. His amber-brown eyes looked clouded and lazy. His thick lips curled downward scornfully, doubt dripping from his expression.

"Am I to understand that you are here under some orders from General Corrington at Fort Rawlins, Mister Holten?" Lieutenant Colonel Waterstratt demanded after the introductions had been made by the sergeant major.

"That's correct," Holten replied drowsily, trying to force some sense out of this nocturnal interview.

"Then, Mister Chief Scout Holten, could you be so kind as to fill me in on the how-as and wherefors of those orders?"

"Uh . . . !" Holten came suddenly wide awake to find himself stuck between a ponderous rock and an exceedingly solid hard place.

Here he was, down in Kansas, because General Corrington's good friend, Capt. Duke Reagan of the Texas Rangers, needed an expert on Plains Indian warfare. Corrington had broken all the rules and had sent Holten, with the full pay and rank of an Army scout. A sudden whimsy provoked Holten to imagine his friend and commander stretched between four powerful draft horses, ready to be quartered by the headsman's axe, while he himself dangled over a low, slow fire, his balls roasting to a meaty-aromaed turn. Holten knew that he must tread lightly or pay dearly as would his good friend, Frank Corrington. He and the general would share their legal vulnerability . . . all the way to the Court of Inquiry and perhaps a court-martial and long, long days at Leavenworth.

"I'm sorry, Colonel." Eli apologized when he

noted the long silence that had followed his first explosive reaction. "About my mission—it was of the utmost secrecy and I regret that I am unable to discuss it with you."

That ought to hold him, Eli thought smugly.

Blandly and with a total lack of apparent guile, the colonel began to discuss a report he had intercepted on the telegraph wire. Addressed to General Corrington, from the commander of Fort Sill, it spoke eloquently of an Eli Holten helping the Texas Rangers put down an uprising of the Kiowa Apaches in the Panhandle of Texas.

"Good work, mind you, but utterly lacking in any legal precedent of the United States Army, or the Public Safety Department of the State of Texas. The whole incident might, to certain picayunish individuals at Department Headquarters, or at the War Department in Washington, even smack of misprision of authority." Waterstratt paused, the scout's smug expression having been magically transferred to his face.

"Oh, well. Never mind. So long as you conduct your duties for the benefit of the *Army*, no such calamitous thoughts could be given birth in anyone's mind. As it happens, I have some work for you right here, Holten. To, ah, justify any pay you might have, er, received while in the service of the Texas Rangers."

What can I do? That thought raced around the suddenly empty cavern of Eli Holten's mind.

For a start, he thought when he calmed down, he could argue the point. General Corrington expected him back. He had already lengthened his stay by diverting to Dodge City when he should have been heading for Kansas City and the sidewheeler packet north to Dakota Territory. However, Lt. Col. Lemuel Waterstratt didn't really look like a man who cared about Eli's problems. He had a problem of his own, obviously.

"Uh . . . what might that be, Colonel?"

"Outlaws. Or, more precisely, a lot of fucking outlaws. Or Indians, if you believe that civilian Bat Masterson."

"And, uh, what am I supposed to do about it?"

"First off, all of my regular scouts are off on two large patrols, riding the line between Colorado and Kansas. They are searching for any renegade Arapaho or Cheyenne who might be responsible for the depredations to local homesteads. Secondly, a series of mysterious raids in the Dodge City area have been plaguing us. To me it appears to be whites. No one has spotted any Cheyenne, Arapaho, Kiowa, or any other goddamned kind of bucks painted up for war, but the Army's hands are tied. I can do no more without someone knowledgeable in the tactics and habits of the plains tribes to scout for my command. Therefore, I would urge you . . ."

A polite Army term for being ordered, Holten thought gloomily.

". . . I would *strongly* urge you to remain here awhile and look into it. I can arrange a wire to Fort Rawlins, informing your commander that you are to be considered TDY to us for the duration of the emergency."

A way out! "Uh . . . is it an emergency, Colonel? An *official* emergency?"

"Ummmm. Ah, n-no. Not as of this minute. But I can assure you, sir, that the danger exists. We could have a full-scale uprising on our hands at any moment. And, of course, there is this little matter of being, ah—lent, is it?—to the Texas Rangers, while on Army pay. Surely, you can find it in you to, ah, take the time to come to our aid?"

"Damn! And I didn't even get a glass of brandy."

"What's that?"

"Oh, nothing, Colonel. Only . . . it always seems that Frank, ah, the general saves the hardest assignments for me. When he's about to spring one on me, I can always tell. He hauls out his premium, twenty-year-old brandy and pours me three fingers. Then he gives me a cigar."

"And you expect this sort of treatment every time the Army demands a bit of work from you?"

"Well, you see, sir . . . ah, I don't mind being screwed. Only . . . I like to get kissed, too."

Susan Faith Walters, nee Meagan, sat primly across from her husband of six hours. Joseph Walters remained silent as he studied the words on a page of the Bible in his lap. His finger traced the lines of the verse and his lips moved slightly as he silently pronounced the words. At last he paused and looked up.

"A pleasant wedding." He offered this comment to his bride.

44

"Uh . . . yes. Yes, it was," Susan returned, with a wisp of a smile. Those were hardly the words she would have chosen, though to be honest, they . . . fit.

Truth to be told, she was experiencing some indecisiveness and a bit of apprehension still haunted her soul. Joseph Walters was a strapping man, fifteen years her senior, thirty-two to her seventeen. Their worlds, she knew, were drastically different. Yet, she should be glad to be married off to such a fine gentleman as Joseph. *Finally married off*, the thought mocked her. She could not hope for better than her Joseph. Still, she didn't love him, not with the burning desire she had dreamed of and longed for all these years.

For his own part, Joseph was fully aware of Susan's longing for romance. A stolid, humorless farmer, a man dedicated first and foremost to the land, he had remained a bachelor until his union with Susan. For him, passion was reserved for the miracle of the planting cycle. Not unfamiliar with womankind and the means to delight them, he was determined to take an especially long time to bring his bride to arousal and satiation. In furtherance of his plan, he now snapped shut the Bible and laid it on a small spool table beside the wide, inviting bed.

"Come, wife," he declared in a deep, rumbling voice, as he raised himself from the chair and gestured toward her with open, welcoming arms. "It is not yet dark, but in honor of our marriage day, my friends have seen to the chores. Now, with

45

the formalities over, but one thing will complete our nuptials." Damn, he cursed himself. Why did he have to make it so ridiculously formal?

Susan winced at his stilted form of address and rose to her feet. Joseph took her in his arms and kissed her gently. His lips left hers to lightly caress her closed eyelids, her cheeks, nose, and the hollow of her throat. He heard the catch in her breath and a responding tightness grew in his loins. Gently he touched her with his gnarled, yet sensitive fingers, feeling through the thick layers of her wedding dress the rapid tattoo of her pounding heart. Slowly his arms encircled her.

With a deftness unexpected by Susan, Joseph began to undo the buttons that traced the length of her spine. Sudden anxiety tightened her firm, youthful body and she gasped at the warm touch of his palm against her bare back. With almost comic gentleness in a man so large, he slid her shoulders free of the lace and damask, peeling it away from her creamy flesh to reveal all the glory of her delightful form. Susan trembled as the dress fell away.

Joseph used greater speed to doff her chemise and petticoats, and then unlaced her corset. Within moments all of her radiant charms had been exposed for his appreciation. And appreciate them he did.

"You are lovely," he murmured.

"I-I . . . don't know . . . what to . . . do." Her voice quavered every bit as much as her body.

"Let me. I . . . I'll guide you," Joseph responded in a tone more tender than that he had used with the casual women of his past or the animals on his farm. He parted from the lovely vision of his bride to light a lamp at the other side of the bed.

Its soft, yellow glow filled the comfortable soddy and sent their figures shadow-dancing on the wall. Quickly, Joseph removed his own clothing. Then he crossed back to where Susan waited. Her eyes had become fixed on the large, swollen object that protruded, bouncing and swaying, from a thatch of dark hair at the juncture of Joseph's thighs. From its encompassing fold of skin, a deep red arrowhead seemed to regard her with its single eye, and it called out to the wild yearning deep in her soul. Susan's breath quickened and her breast heaved with frightened anticipation. Joseph knelt before her and warmly kissed her taut belly.

Susan shivered as Joseph's fluttering lips worked lower, across the swell of her lower abdomen and down into the bristly thatch of strawberry hair that covered her hot, pulsating mound. Nuzzling, like a pony after sugar, Joseph stimulated the outer portals of her untried cavern until he had teased it open in tingling invitation. Then he began to explore the fronds of her cave with his tongue.

"Eeiiii!" Susan keened, experiencing for the first time one of the greatest delights a man can give. "I . . . I feel faint, Joseph. Oh . . . oh . . . oh, wha-what are you doing to me?"

"Open your eyes, dearest, and see." His rumbling words further stimulated that virgin purse and a wellspring of sweet nectar flowed from deep within her.

Hard, work-worn hands located the portals and spread them wide, so that Joseph could plunge further within. Pleasure-formed electric shocks ran through the beautiful redhead's slender frame and she lost her nervousness as nature took command of her body. Slowly her hips began to oscillate and pump back and forth, her juices running as freely now that they smeared Joseph's cheeks as he endeavored to bury his face further into the perfumed salon of delights.

He located the tiny bud of her snail-of-many-joys and nipped at it playfully with his teeth. Susan shrieked out her happiness and pressed both hands to the back of Joseph's head. He continued to lap at her unending fountain until she began to whine and gyrate in delirious abandon.

As the thunderous crash of her first nonself-induced climax inundated her, Joseph rose and guided her to the bed. There he arranged her and lay at her side, end for end. Before his head sank between her thighs once more, he spoke tenderly, encouragingly.

"Take it, Susan. Take it in, my love."

Susan looked at the large, blue-veined organ that thrust toward her face, only inches away. Her eyes went wide at the prospect, but her mouth and tongue knew what to do without conscious direction.

One small hand drew back the loose skin that

housed his slightly flattened tip and her tongue darted out to circle it, teasingly. She felt his trembling response and gathered her courage for more. With a sudden jerk forward, she enclosed his raging member in the warm, moist confines of her mouth.

Oh, how good this was, she thought as she continued to lick and suck. From the vibrations of Joseph's body she knew it had an equally delightful effect on him. If only this could last forever, Susan's raging mind sang joyously.

Got to make it last, Joseph cautioned himself. Give her everything she wants, sooth her and make the final act so desperately wanted she will never notice the moment's pain when she parts with her maidenhead. She must lust for it, beg for it. Cry out in happiness. Then . . . although she is not aware her secret is known, all reservations will be gone and love will come in its time. How marvelously she does that, he exclaimed to himself as his tongue delved even deeper into her musky passage.

Sudden noises from outside interrupted their happy interlude. Joseph paused, body silently rigid, listening. When the sounds were repeated, he knew the greatest terror of the remote homesteader. Someone had broken into his barn. The stock was being herded out. Quickly he rose from the bed.

"What is it?" Susan whispered, caught by the urgency her husband's tense face revealed.

"I don't know. Could be renegades."

"I-Indians?"

"I'm afraid so, Susan."

Still naked, Joseph padded to a window and peered out.

In the gathering gloom of twilight, he saw forms flitting from place to place. They wore white men's clothing and boots, though here and there he saw a decorated feather sprouting from the sweat band of a dirty Stetson or a dome-peaked, black, trade hat. Automatically, Joseph's hand reached for his rifle. Then he recalled his bride of so few hours.

"Quick, get out of bed. Wrap up in something."

"Why? Who's out there?"

"Don't ask questions. Do as I say."

Quickly Susan climbed from the bed where she had been so happy only moments before. She pulled on a light cotton wrapper and belted it, sliding her feet into small canvas slippers.

"What do I do now?"

"Come with me."

In the main room of the soddy, Joseph went to a cleverly hidden bolt hole and opened the camouflaged cover. "Get in there, Susan. Hurry. And . . . no matter what you hear, stay there. Don't open this door. If . . . if anything happens, fire or such, there is a short tunnel. You can kick it open with your feet. Crawl through it to the cottonwoods by the creek. Then wait there until you are sure it is safe. Don't show yourself for any reason."

"Where will you be?"

"I . . . I won't matter then."

50

"You'll be dead!" Susan wailed.

"Yes, beloved. I will. But you must live. Hide until it is safe to go to Dodge City. You may have to walk, so take along stout shoes." Joseph left off his instructions to return to the bedroom and obtain a heavy pair of work brogans. "These will do. Now, lay down and be quiet as you can. I . . . I love you, dear Susan."

"I love you, too, my Joseph. Please . . . don't let anything happen. Please . . ."

The hidden trap door closed over her and she found herself in darkness. She could hear enough, though. Violent pounding on the sent shivers of fright through her body, where a minute ago passion had burned brightly.

A loud report from Joseph's rifle nearly m her cry out in alarm. Only a hand over her mout insured silence. The pounding continued, accompanied by piercing war whoops and more shots. A splintering crash told her the door had been breached. More shots followed and two bodies hit the floor above. Then more rounds were discharged. She heard a scream, prolonged and agonized, then a moment's silence. Harsh, strange voices grunted words she could not understand, and there were shuffling footsteps as the soddy got a thorough search. Then silence again.

Susan heard the distant crackling long before she realized what it meant. It grew in volume and she felt a wave of warmth pass over her reclining body. Then she smelled the smoke.

Desperately, she began to kick at the thin

partition of dirt that separated her from the tunnel. Dry and hard from lack of rain, the earth stubbornly refused to budge. She drew up her knees and kicked harder.

Something gave. With building panic, Susan smashed at the first cave-in, despite her flagging strength determined to break through—not to perish. At last she could move into the escape passage.

In a niche carved into one wall, she felt the outlines of an old paper cartridge musket. With it she found a box of loads, percussion caps, and a canteen, empty, but otherwise ready for a journey. A small roll of cured deer hide provided some strips of jerky. Slowly, her heart sick over the certainty of her husband's death, she began to inch her way along the tunnel.

"I'll need some troops with me," Eli remarked when he and Lieutenant Colonel Waterstratt met again the next morning after Officers' Call. "I can't single-handedly do everything you're asking of me."

"Of course, Scout. There are some infantry you can use."

"How? If I'm slowed to their pace, the whole of this end of the state can be wiped clean of white settlement before we come within sight of whoever is doing it."

"Oh, we'll find transporation for them, be sure of that."

"Infantrymen on horseback?" Eli scoffed. "Nelson Miles tried that out at Fort Kearny. Didn't work out all that well."

"No!" Waterstratt exclaimed, apparently sincerely offended by the idea that good Army horses should be sullied by the posteriors of infantrymen. "Not horses, Mister Holten. Just . . . transportation."

Chapter Four

A little after noontime chow, the same day the scout got his new assignment, Sergeant Major O'Brannigan found Eli Holten in the sutler's store. The scout stood at the bar, his powerful, long-fingered hand wrapped around a beer schooner, an empty whiskey glass at its side.

"Ah, an' there ye are, Mister Holten," O'Brannigan said cheerily. "The colonel's compliments, sir, an' your expedition is all tricked out and waitin' far ye outside headquarters."

"Thank you, Sergeant Major. Only . . . isn't it a bit late in the day to start a reconnaissance patrol?"

"Not by the lights of Lt. Col. Lemuel Waterstratt, it isn't. The first place what was hit is not far from here. Ye can be makin' camp beyond it before nightfall."

"I'm overjoyed," Eli returned drily.

"Lt. Richard Stone will be commandin'. An' as a special favor to you, I'm goin' to send along my best troop sergeant, Clerance O'Kelly. He'll keep those foot sloggers in line, ridin' or not, sir."

"What are these mounts, Sergeant Major?"

"Ah . . . better be gittin' out there, Mister Holten. Ye'll be seein' 'em soon enough, I'd allow.

Holten sauntered out onto the porch of the sutler's store. There he stopped abruptly, his mouth sagging, eyes bugging from their sockets. Slowly, disbelievingly, he turned his head to take in the mounted column.

Mules.

An entire platoon of infantry sat astride a mixed bag of blacks and grays. The animals' long, jackrabbit ears were perked up, their tails swaying defiantly. Sitting astride the ugliest mule Eli had ever seen was a soldier dressed in the uniform of a lieutenant. He seemed to be trying to hold onto the last vestige of his pride as well as the reins of his . . . mount.

Eli, a man who liked to burst into gales of unrestrained laughter if the moment warranted, could not contain himself at this unnatural spectacle. He had lost his control in past situations when someone wiser might have tried to suppress joviality. This proved to be one of those times.

Sergeant Major O'Brannigan stood, red-faced, while the scout strolled across the parade ground, laughing until tears came to his eyes, blinding him so that he staggered. Holten howled at the ludicrous spectacle of a platoon of foot soldiers straddling these silly-looking creatures. Ultimately, as the stern, top NCO of Fort Dodge watched in anguish, Holten, wiping his streaming eyes, stumbled into the legs of one mule. He looked up and instantly fell silent.

Colonel Lemuel Waterstratt sat astride his mule, chewing at a cigar, contemplating Holten.

"Having our little joke, are we?" the colonel demanded icily.

"Uh . . . well, that is . . . yes, sir. That's what we were doing."

"You find these infantrymen mounted on mules humorous?"

"I—"

"I came down to see the platoon off, Mister Holten. I had hoped that you would have the good sense to leave your horse behind and take one of the Army mules. I gather, from your reaction to the sight of *my* favorite means of transportation, that you would prefer your Morgan, eh, Mister Holten?"

"Uh . . . Yes, sir. That I do. Sonny and I have been together a long time. Wouldn't seem the same without him. And . . . he'd pine for me, too, sir."

"Ridiculous." The colonel sniffed. "However, it would no doubt have an effect on your usefulness. So, proceed, Mister Holten. Proceed."

Eli went to the tie rail where he had left Sonny saddled and loaded with field gear. He stepped into the stirrups and nodded to the green-looking young lieutenant.

"Column of twos to the left," Lieutenant Stone commanded. "Ho!"

The platoon swung into formation and ambled, at the mule version of a walk, out the main gate. With a lot of goading and kicking, they developed a fairly brisk pace. The course led to the northwest.

"Yaaaaeeee!" one female victim shrieked as the partly naked man kneeling between her thighs slashed her throat. Her dying tremors brought him to a quick completion and he ejaculated in a white gush into the quivering wreckage of her vagina.

"Good!" he grunted as he rose, squeezing his turgid penis dry. "Good that way."

The other women who had gathered in the soddy for protection had died with only whimpers or moans. All had been raped repeatedly. Three small, naked boys, aged eight to twelve, had been savagely sodomized. Now it became their turn to die as well. The oldest lad still retained a spark of defiance.

When a raggedly dressed half-breed rolled him over and grasped his white-blond hair to pull back his head for a clean throat cut, the boy kicked his assailant in the testicles. A howl of agony blubbered from the renegade's lips and he dropped his knife to clutch his aching scrotum.

"Let him live," Charlie Roundtree snapped as the others moved in menacingly. "Why you do that, boy? You hurt in hole?"

"Th' buggerin' didn't hurt all that much," the child piped up. "But he did bad things to my maw an' kilt her. That's not right. If . . . if I had a gun, I'd shoot him dead."

Charlie smiled, impressed by the boy's courage. "This is war. People die in war."

"It's not the same," the youngster snapped back. "Soldiers fight in a war. They expect to get killed. Not women an' kids."

"Did we not fight like soldiers? Use bugle calls?"

"Uh . . . yes."

"Not like Injuns?"

"Uh . . . no."

"Then we soldiers, this war."

"Uh . . . yes."

"You tell other whites about war," Charlie demanded. "Tell 'em we fight them until they leave. You go now."

Behind Charlie, his men labored to load the stacks of loot aboard two buckboards. They hooted and yelled, passing among them the three crockery jugs of powerful homemade whiskey which had been located in the barn. Charlie glanced at them, then at the corpses that littered the ground.

"Can . . . can I get some clothes?" the boy requested.

Charlie gazed at his naked body for a moment and smiled. "Take shirt. Nothing else. Trousers make hole hurt more."

"I . . . uh, thanks," the boy managed before he began to cry over the murder of his mother and brothers. He rubbed grubby knuckles into his eyes and turned away to locate a shirt.

Once the excess booty had been secured on the raiding party's horses, the column formed up and rode away. At the top of a long, gentle swale,

Charlie Roundtree reined in.

"Coohooty Smith," he told one of his lieutenants, "I must go back. There is something that I want at the soddy."

"We took everything, Charlie. You saw that."

"No. I see what I want and hide. Go back now."

As the disciplined renegades continued on their way, Charlie Roundtree cantered back to the farmyard. There he dismounted and walked to the prone body of the eight-year-old. He knelt and picked up the corpse. Rising, he strode to his horse and loaded his burden. Then he swung into the saddle and rode off, heading away from Dodge City and from his own men.

Huge, black, cruciform shapes hovered in the hot afternoon air. Circling lazily, they formed a perfect beacon for Eli Holten to follow. At a lope, Sonny closed the ground until the scout saw in the distance the smudged outline of a low-lying soddy. More buzzards hung heavily in the sky over the silent homestead. Holten's keen eyes took in the particulars and he turned his mount back toward the advancing column of mule-borne infantry.

"There's a place up ahead, Lieutenant," Eli told Stone. "About two miles. Buzzards are thick. I thought this happened a week or more ago?"

"The attack we knew about did. This one has to be new. Family name of Tadlock live over that way. That's all I know."

Fifteen minutes later, with Holten and Lieutenant Stone in the lead, the small column trotted into

59

the farmyard. Indolently, each flap of wing and squawk of protest displaying eloquent arrogance, the buzzards rose from gorging themselves on the remains of the Tadlocks. Several soldiers became sick and slid from their mounts to vomit in the baked dust of the farmyard.

Eli walked over to the corral, where he peered down at two bodies, that of a man and a woman. Not far away, a boy in his early teens lay in a welter of blood, the back of his skull bashed in by some heavy, blunt object.

"Sergeant O'Kelly," Stone called out.

"Sir!"

"Form a burial detail. We'll look around a bit." To Holten, he remarked, "How long ago do you think this happened?"

"From the way the buzzards have been at 'em, and the coyote tracks, I'd say early yesterday . . . maybe the day before."

"This makes eleven all together. We have to find whoever is doing this and stop it quick. There'll be a panic."

"It has all the markings of an Indian raid, Lieutenant," Eli went on as they walked around the yard, eyes on the ground. The scout and the officer stopped by the burned-out barn. "Yet . . . that's all we have. It *looks* like Indians did it."

"How do you mean?"

"What do you see on the ground? Is there a single moccasin print here?"

"Uh . . . no," Stone replied after a quick sweep of the mingled tracks.

"See any arrows, or wounds in the corpses that

could have come from an arrow or a lance?''

"Now that you mention it . . . no.''

"Would white folk, who already feared Indian attack, remain out in the yard, unarmed like these people were, if they saw Indians coming?''

"Maybe the savages snuck up on them?''

"How, Lieutenant?'' Eli swung his arm in a wide arc. "They would have had to fall out of the sky to make a sneak attack. Those boot prints— shod horses. Even using a pair of wagons to take off who knows what. All that points to white renegades. Are there any holdovers from the Red Legs hanging out around here? What do they call themselves now? Ku Kluxers? Or maybe some of John Brown's Abolitionist fanatics? It appears to me it could be some of that kind's work.''

"Sir,'' Richard Stone informed Eli Holten in a stiff, offended tone. "I'll have you know I had the honor and distinction of serving in the recent conflict as a drummer boy in an Ohio Volunteer Regiment. The Two-fifty-first, as a matter of fact. That got me my appointment later on to the Academy.''

Eli cracked an easy, amused smile. "Relax, Lieutenant. I am not an unreconstructed Rebel. I was out beyond the Black Hills, living with the Sioux during that war. Didn't even know it had happened until it was over. It's just that fanatics— of any stripe—tend to be a lot more brutal and bloodier than ordinary fighting men.''

"I, ah, beg your pardon, sir. And, uh, if you please, call me Rick.''

"Sure, Rick. And I'm Eli.''

For the first time since the patrol had left Fort Dodge, Richard Stone smiled. "We had better hurry up that burial detail, Eli. We've a lot of ground to cover yet."

Stone appeared to be only five or so years younger than Eli, although short-cropped blond hair and cold gray-blue eyes suggested someone much older. His revelations about serving with the Union Army during the War Between the States could account for his calm acceptance of the horrors they had discovered here. Stone was wiry, Holten noticed, and a bit taller than the scout, which made him look all the more ludicrous on a mule. Despite his early service, though, one could easily tell that he had only begun to learn how to fight Indians. But a quick learner, Eli allowed. And apparently not afraid of much in this world. He had a scar that started behind his ear and worked its way down half of his cheek. Mutton-chop sideburns hid most of it, but Eli wondered how the lieutenant had gotten it. As though he had been reading Eli's mind, Sgt. Clerance O'Kelly stepped over to the scout and spoke quietly.

"If ye be wonderin' about the good lieutenant, sir, I kin set yer mind at ease. He's as tough as they come, outta West Point that is. An' older than most of the shavetails. He picked up that scar durin' the war. That's all any of us know about it."

Ten more minutes passed before the soldiers mounted and rode out of the demolished home-stead. They continued onward for a good hour. Up ahead, Eli Holten signaled for the column to approach at a gallop. When they arrived, they saw yet another ruined farmstead. In the yard, near a clump of cottonwoods, a young woman labored to move large stones from a pile and place them neatly on a mound of freshly turned dirt. She wore some sort of lightweight house robe and her strands of pinkish, strawberry blond hair kept straying into her face. At the sound of hoofs, she stopped her labors and snatched up an old muzzle-loading percussion musket.

"Stand where you are!" she called out.

"It's the United States Army, ma'am," Richard Stone responded.

"Where were you when we needed you?"

"Uh . . . sorry, ma'am. When were you attacked?"

"Late afternoon, day before yesterday."

"May we ride in closer?"

"Uh . . . sure. Pardon the gun, but you understand, don't you?"

"Of course we do."

Once the troops had gathered and dismounted, Lieutenant Stone introduced himself, Eli Holten, and Sgt. Clerance O'Kelly.

"I am Susan Meagan, er, Walters that is. Even though I was only married six hours before . . . before my . . . husband . . . was killed." Tears accompanied the words Susan choked out, for the first time revealing her deep and abiding grief.

Richard Stone hastened to console the widow, only to have her turn toward Eli Holten for support. The hot flare of jealousy that rose in the lieutenant's breast died down when he saw the stricken, helpless expression on the scout's face. Clumsily, Eli patted Susan's shaking shoulders, and murmured words of sympathy and encouragement. At last her sobbing subsided and she wiped at her eyes.

"Pardon me, ma'am, at a time like this. But . . . there's another homestead, about ten miles southeast of you. I believe it was the Tadlocks. . . ." Miserably, Stone let it hang, the implication all too clear.

"Was? You mean . . . they have been wiped out too? All four of them?"

"Four, ma'am?" the lieutenant inquired anxiously.

"Why, yes. They were here for the wedding. Absalom and Audrey, Steven, and little Rebecca."

"The girl? How old was she?"

"Uh . . . I believe her mother said she had just turned eleven. Why, Lieutenant?"

"We, ah, found only three bodies."

"Then . . . then Rebecca must have wandered off somewhere? She could still be alive?"

"It's a possibility, Miz Walters," Richard Stone offered uncomfortably. Then Eli Holten brutally finished the thought for him.

"Or the raiders took her off with them." Susan's face turned white but the scout ignored it, pressing on to his point. "Their place had been hit before yours. Did you happen to hear any sound of a child. Screams or a voice?"

"N-no. I didn't hear anything like that. Would

that mean they killed Rebecca and threw her poor body away on the prairie?''

"Not necessarily. It gives us more hope. There's a chance she might still be alive and free of their clutches.''

"Oh . . . oh, Mister Holten, do you think that is possible?''

"Anything is possible, Miz Walters.''

Hope bloomed. "This is the nearest place,'' Susan went on, thinking it out aloud. "If . . . if Rebecca survived the attack, she would head here. Oh, it may be that she will still show up. It's getting quite late, Lieutenant Stone, Mister Holten. Why don't you and your men put up here for the night. Then, if Rebecca is out there somewhere, she might come in when she sees fires and hears voices. Oh!'' A hand flew to her mouth.

"What is it?'' Stone asked, sensing something relevant.

"The men who attacked us. They spoke in English and they wore white men's clothes. My husband told me the last part. I heard them talking while I hid in the special compartment Joseph had prepared for emergencies. So . . . so your appearance might frighten her away.''

"We'll have to stay anyway, Miz Walters,'' Lieutenant Stone said gently. "Either here or a short distance away. It's too near sunset now. And . . . you'll have to come along with us until we find some other settlers or take you back to Fort Dodge.''

"But this is my home,'' Susan protested.

"Is it?" Eli reminded her roughly as he cast an arm to take in the burned-out soddy, smoldering barn, and demolished chicken pen.

"Oh . . . oh, my God!" Susan sobbed anew as she buried her face in her hands. "What shall I do? Whatever shall I do?"

Chapter Five

By the time the mules had been picketed and wood gathered for cook fires, Eli and Susan had reached a first-name basis. The light voices of the soldiers drifted through the waning afternoon, accompanied by the redolent odors of cooking beans and bacon, and brewing coffee. The scout walked with the young widow some distance from the center of activity. Their course took them along the willow-shrouded bank of a creek that fed into the distant Arkansas River. The meandering water looked cool and inviting.

"I . . . This might sound strange, Eli," Susan said through a sigh. "But I would like a bath. I've done nothing but dig for a whole day and bury poor Joseph. I must smell frightfully of wood smoke and dank earth." She examined her smudged hands and arms as she spoke.

"You don't look all that, ah, disheveled, Susan," Eli offered gallantly.

"All the same, I feel as damaged on the outside as I do on the inside." This time her sigh was weighted with the deprivation she felt because of the untimely termination of her first encounter with her husband. Was she always to remain a virgin?

"You must have loved your husband very much," Eli remarked as he observed her deep sorrow.

"I . . . I can't really say that," Susan responded in another pain-filled exhalation. "I . . . hardly had a chance to know the man, Eli."

"Oh? How is that?"

"Didn't you know? We had only been married a matter of hours when the . . . when those men came." A sudden, powerful stirring of the vital sap that had started to rise in her maidenly veins drove Susan to boldness. "Why, in fact, we had not even, er, consummated the marriage." She turned toward the scout, her eyes shining with an amorous light, and clasped one of his large hands in both of hers.

"You know, I think I really should have that bath before the sun goes down." She emphasized her meaning by nodding toward the west, where a fat, red sun hung a hand's breadth above the horizon. Then she chattered on.

"I haven't any soap or a towel, the fire destroyed all that. But the warm air will dry me and . . . with you to keep watch, I wouldn't be disturbed. . . ."

She left her enthusiastic proposition hanging for Eli to fasten upon.

"I have both in my saddlebags. Why don't you, ah, prepare yourself while I fetch them? Then you can clean yourself at your leisure while I keep an eye on the soldiers."

"Would you?" Susan gushed. "That would be marvelous. Oh, thank you, Eli."

With no more urging, Eli hurried off to obtain the soap and a large square of rough toweling material he carried along for those occasions when he must needs clean himself before appearing in public after a long time on the prairie. Distantly, he felt a familiar, though unexpected stirring in his loins. He found that the efficient Sergeant O'Kelly had posted sentries and established a duty roster for the night. Boundaries had been drawn, beyond which the troops would not venture except under pain of severe punishment.

The Army had abolished flogging, but it still allowed a miscreant to be spread-eagled and lashed, bare to the waist, over the hub of a wagon wheel, either horizontally or vertically. Many a minor offender had found himself digging a hole, six by six by six, with a large mess-hall spoon, only to be commanded to fill it in again. Ultimately, for the worst violators, there was the military prison at Fort Leavenworth, Kansas—or the gallows. To avoid any or all of these, the soldiers went to great lengths to follow regulations and obey the orders of their officers and noncoms. The arrangement made by O'Kelly pleased Eli as he dug into Sonny's saddlebags.

Good, he thought. That keeps the creek well outside the limits. He retrieved the objects he sought and walked back to the concealing bower of willows. There he found Susan sitting demurely, though stark naked, upon a scant pile of clothing. She smiled up at his momentary astonishment.

"I told you how little Joseph and I knew each other. Yet, in the small time we had together, he lit something in me I can't deny. It . . . makes me ache like I haven't eaten in a week." Susan patted a spot beside her and framed her features into a coy, though inviting, expression.

"Why don't you take off your clothes and join me, Eli? Then we could both be refreshed."

The scout spread the blanket and hastened to comply.

Already his mighty loaf had begun to rise, as though leavened by the most powerful of yeast. Its bulge could be seen in the straining cloth of his trousers, which he quickly doffed. Susan's breath quickened at the sight and her gaze remained fixed upon the use-browned device that swayed before her enraptured eyes. Oh, her thrilled mind rang gleefully, this was much more like how she had dreamed it would be. A tall, handsome man with . . . with enough of what it took to make a girl come apart at the seams.

It's not food she's in need of, Eli knew when he saw her heart pounding against her delicate, creamy flesh. Like a bird penned in a covered cage, the small organ of life fluttered in a vain attempt to break free.

70

"You see, Eli," Susan went on in her soft, intriguing voice, "we never got to finish. Not even once." Her hands went out to greedily grasp his throbbing organ, to gently manipulate it. "When I think about it, I hurt so bad I nearly double over. After I got over my fear and grief, I began to wonder how, now that I am a widow, I would ever learn the sweet mysteries that Joseph promised to introduce me to. Then, when . . . when I saw you, I . . . knew how."

Eli sighed heavily. He didn't want to interrupt the excellent entertainment this starving young widow was lavishing upon him, but certain sensibilities could better be catered to if they both smelled fresher. "Susan, don't you think we should get that bath first?"

"First?" she asked in youthful innocence. "Before . . . what?"

A smile creased the scout's firm lips. "Before we see about feeding you."

Crystal bells tinkled in Susan's girlish laughter. She let go of his roasting flesh and rose gracefully.

Eli could well appreciate the desirable shape that stood like a wood nymph before him. Graceful curves announced her recent entry into womanhood. Her breasts, though smaller than many, stood pert and proud, the pink nipples upthrust and already hardening. Her long, strawberry hair hung in silken tresses that fell capelike over her shoulders, covering them with a dignity that no raiment could imitate. She held her shoulders straight, which only emphasized the arch and flare of her rib cage; the delightful slope to her small, round belly; the dimple of her navel; and the arrow-point plunge from her burgeoning hips to her furry valley of delights.

There, a small thatch barely covered her swollen mound. Framed by sculptured thighs, that pouch of great promise beckoned the scout's inspection. Yet he refrained and joined her in stepping into the warm water of the sandy-bottomed creek. Eli still held the soap, once she had ducked down to wet her body all over, from behind he began to lather her shoulders. His ponderous plentitude pressed against the top of the dividing cleft of her buttocks and she wiggled backward against it to find and enjoy greater pleasure.

"Wash me here," she commanded, delicately touching his firming nipples of her youthful breasts. "Ah, yes. That's it. Oh, that's so much better than doing it for yourself. Rub harder, Eli. Ooooh, that's fine. So very fine. Now work around here a little . . . and here . . . and there . . . that's it. Lower . . . lower . . . Eiii! That's where . . . where Joseph and I were when the attack came. Rub some more. Yes . . . yes . . . oh . . . *yes*!"

With practiced ease, Eli washed the girl. By the time he finished, both were panting with effort and arousal. On the western horizon, a mighty blaze of color spread upward. Subtle bands and rays of pastel pink, blue, and lemon vied with deeper bars of purple, scarlet, and black. The earth seemed to tremble at the magnificence of the sunset.

"Oh . . . it's so beautiful," Susan managed to gasp out.

They rinsed and climbed from the water, glowing with health and stimulation. Susan lay on the towel, her eyes hooded by dreams, arms and legs spread in invitation. Eli knelt beside her and recalled her earlier words. Slowly he stretched out beside her and with deft fingers worked to prepare a feast to slake her inner hunger.

Deep in the petals of her bower, he located her harmonious *escargot* and began to tweak it, kindling her passion and igniting a flame in the hearth of Susan's heart. With competent strokes, he fanned the slight glow of her desire until it burst, hot, yet moist with its lambent fuel. Meanwhile she began to knead the dough of his stalwart loaf, raising it to even higher peaks of achievement. He realized she could no longer control her hunger as she bent to sample his staff of life.

Wave after wave of delicious sensation washed over the scout as Susan fed upon his richness, working it ever more deeply within as though to consume him all. She made tiny sounds of happiness as she licked the surface in search of the frosting. Her hips began to undulate and she moaned, making him aware that her desperation came not so much from a desperation to eat, as to be eaten. Quickly he replaced his fingers with his lips.

Sweet nectar flowed onto his tongue as he worked it into the narrow confines of her bakery shop. There he sampled the diverse sweets laid out for his inspection. A little of this . . . a bit of that . . . some of the cream tart and a generous portion of fiery furnace. Susan squealed in ecstasy as Eli's meal progressed. Ravenous herself now, she strove to improve her ability to feast upon his warm and fragrant loaf.

Their meal of many pleasures had hardly started, yet both healthy young bodies vibrated with the urgency to consume even more. With gluttonous determination, Susan swallowed the last bit of Eli's ample excess to prove her famished state. Yet, they had only browsed among the appetizers at their amorous banquet table.

When at last the cauldron simmered near the edge of boiling, Holten deftly brought the girl-woman around and positioned her above his supine frame, lowering her spicy pouch over his flame-warmed skewer.

Slowly she descended, her already warm vessel opening wide to receive the instrument of its searing. Her first contact, wet and ready, thrilled them both. A deeper stirring of the broth met with momentary resistance. Released at last amid the viands of love, Susan strove mightily to dispense with that small impediment to full gourmet enjoyment.

It burst with a tiny knifing pain and she threw back her head to howl silently in acceptance of her new status. Slowly the rigid ladle began to stir the passionate stew, swirling, twisting, delving deeper to roil the luscious fruits that comprised this awesome dish. All too soon the first course ended in a shower of heady wine that, for the moment, banked the fires of Susan's oven.

"Now . . ." Susan panted softly into the dark

dome of sky above, "now I know what I nearly had. Don't ever take it away, Eli. This was only a first time, but a most wonderful one for me. I . . . I could do that forever. You make me feel complete."

"There'll be other times," the scout promised, mindful of how exhausting and demanding this lovely creature had proven to be. Yes. He could hardly abandon this prize of prizes to other, coarser, and untutored hands without at least another buffet supper.

A thick stand of cottonwoods turned the wide, lazy bend of the Arkansas River into a verdant park. Grass had managed to take root in the mixture of sand, loam, and mulch that littered the area, so that the harsh, desertlike country to the south of Dodge City became a natural campsite with an ample screen of trees to insure privacy. There a gathering of low, skin lodges; brush shelters; and canvas tents housed the renegade army of Charlie Roundtree. In the crisp morning light, smoke from wood fires rose in lazy spirals among the branches overhead, and the delightful aroma of cooking buffalo and boiling coffee tantalized Charlie's nostrils.

He stood to one side, near the water's edge. From this vantage point, he looked over his men. Most were digging through the booty they had stolen from the soddies and small frame farmhouses they had hit in the past weeks. Much of it consisted of household goods, which on the surface were worthless, but which eventually could be resold to new settlers. Those of his troops who had brought their wives along squatted by the lodge fires, waiting to break their fast. Beyond them, from a stand of trees, came cries of pain and the whimpering sounds of struggle. Some of his band were indulging their lust on the bodies of young captives brought along to be so used.

These white girls, ranging in age from eleven to sixteen, had been forced into the traditional role of captives in an Indian camp. Slaves. As Charlie listened in amusement, the moans of terror gradually became groans of hunger, and the cries of pain changed into the keening of exquisite pleasure as the girls gave themselves over to the enjoyment of the rigid lances that slithered in and out of their tender, and now willing, young bodies. It had been so with all of their captives, Charlie mused. They started out fighting and ended up begging for more cock than his band had the endurance to provide. One pair, he recalled delightfully, twin sisters of twelve or so, had become so enflamed and insatiable that they had taken on all sixty of his men, twice, in a prolonged session of uninhibited sexual carnival.

The orgy had lasted two days and a night. Charlie, as was his right as leader, had visited both girls three times. Then had come the memorable conclusion when both naked sprites had slithered all over him, bringing forth a fiery response like none he had experienced before. Hard as a stone pillar he had entered one twin.

"More!" she cried. "More . . . more . . . balls

and all . . . balls and all!''

Charlie churned his buttocks and drove his one-eyed steed deep into her slippery pasture while her sister watched avidly and slid a greased buffalo horn far in and out of her dripping passage. When the explosive end came, the girls had switched, not even giving Charlie time to go limp from the first combat. And so they had continued this incredible marathon all of the second night.

It had left Charlie weak and shaken, unable even to crawl from his tipi when next the sun rose. They lived now in his lodge, and though they could never be satisfied with a single man and freely shared their innumberable charms with all of the band, they saved their most delicious activities for Charlie. His member stiffening at the thought, Charlie looked in the direction of his dwelling and rubbed at the constantly sore lance that ached to get free of his trousers and frolic in the fields of youthful ambition. As he licked dry lips and contemplated a bit of midmorning sport, one of his lieutenants, Joe Sureshot, walked up.

Joe shook his head sadly at the lecherous music being made among the cottonwoods. "We're fooling ourselves if we expect to run the Army out with this gang of ne'er-do-wells," he told his leader. "All they want to do is drink and fuck."

"Can you think of anything better to do?"

A rueful grimace replaced Joe's glower. "No. Not really."

"Well then," Charlie responded brightly. "We might be a band of worthless half-breed scum, but we're faster and meaner than any blue-belly soldier that ever came West. We'll do all right, be sure of that. When the homesteaders leave, the Army won't be far behind. We have the money and supplies behind us to be certain of it. Why, if we wanted one, I think I could even promote a Gatling gun for us."

"You're serious?" Joe's eyes widened, then closed down in contemplation. "I think you are. Tell me, where do we strike next?"

Charlie Roundtree took a rolled map from the waistband of his trousers and opened it. "Here. See these little crosses on the map? Each one is a farm or ranch. They run in an arc this way toward Great Bend. Once we strike there the panic will spread. The whites will sell at any price and leave the land behind. But we must move swiftly. At the moment, all of the Army scouts who are capable of tracking us are off with two large patrols along the Colorado border. So long as the foot soldiers are tied down at Fort Dodge, we are free to do all the harm we wish."

"And once the land is empty, the buffalo will come back?" Joe Sureshot asked sarcastically.

"I'm not idiot enough to believe that old man's dream. We can't keep the whites out forever. They will return, and in force. But we'll have the stores and the land offices. They will have to buy dry goods from us, land from us, farm machinery and livestock from us. We'll be rich, Joe. Richer than any half-breed has ever dreamed of being before." Charlie stopped abruptly and turned toward a wild and disreputable looking white man lounging under the shade of a cottonwood, a cane fishing pole held loosely in one hand.

"Denver!" Charlie snapped. "Sound 'Assembly'."

At once the renegade squawman leaped to his feet and produced a battered, though shiny, regulation bugle. He put it to his lips and blew the staccato notes of the call. Smiling, Charlie turned to Joe.

"You see? They're falling in in perfect files. Every man jack of them rigid at attention. Discipline is the key, Joe. Trust me. We aren't howling savages fighting for glory and *coups*. We're an army in our own right. We'll win because we're doing it the right way."

Chapter Six

"Sure an' we've picked a terrible time to be in this place," Sgt. Clerance O'Kelly whispered in an aside to Eli Holten as the column of mule-soldiers rode into the farmyard. Five stalwart homesteaders faced them, rifles in hand and faces livid with rage.

"Where were you damned blue-bellies when we needed you?" one farmer growled, addressing his complaint to Lieutenant Stone.

"How do you mean, sir?" the green young lieutenant responded.

"*Donkey*-soldiers it is now," another scoffed. "By God, it's no wonder they couldn't get here when we got hit yeste'day."

"Hit by whom?" Stone demanded. "What happened?"

"Three men wounded! Two dead!" the first

man shouted. "That's what we mean. They come right in here in broad daylight. At first we thought it was the Army comin' when we heard the bugle calls. Caught us right in the open it did. Whole big passel of renegade mixed-breeds an' whites. 'Least the one with the horn was white. Kilt Caleb an' Nehemiah right off. Then Absalom got a bullet in the underpinnin's. We fought 'em. Oh, hell yes. You can count on that. Didn't have no choice. Not with the Army off playin' grab-ass with a bunch of stubborn mules."

"They got Norton an' Hayes next an' ran off all our stock. We don't dare even go back to our own places now, what with the horses stolen an' our numbers cut down. What if they come back?"

"Well"—Lieutenant Stone mollified them—"we're here now. We'll remain for as long as possible. But our mission is to find those raiders and bring them to justice."

"Justice, hell!" a third sodbuster snapped. "What they need is a taste of the hemp. Next you know, they'll be takin' our womenfolk."

"Not so long as we are here . . . Mister?"

"Deines. Milton Deines. Look here, soldier boy, are you gonna escort us to our homes? Leave some of these blue-suits to protec' what's ours?"

"Sorry, we can't do that. We're headed after the renegades. And we have to stop by Dodge City. If any of you wish to accompany us that far, we'll be glad to make arrangements," Lieutenant Stone informed the gathered men. Behind them, women and children came timidly from a fortified soddy, eyes wide with fear, reluctant even in the face of

81

these soldiers to show themselves to possible danger. "Otherwise, there's nothing we can do," the young officer added apologetically. "Now, what can you tell us about these raiders?"

"Like we said, they used bugle calls, an' fired in volleys—advanced in ranks like reg'lar troops." Milton Deines reviewed his earlier statements. "But they whooped and hollered like Injuns. They wore white men's clothes, though."

"Half-breeds," Holten suggested, recalling an earlier statement.

"Coulda been. Weren't no feathers or other tribal markings," the first farmer allowed.

"Then definitely not a Cheyenne raiding party, or the Kiowa on the warpath?" the scout asked.

"Nope. Not like that at all."

"Perhaps only a lot of human maggots running amok on the countryside, then?"

Deines looked askance at the scout for a moment, considering what Holten had said. "Maybe," he conceded at last. "Or maybe a regular uprisin' by the mixed-bloods. I've heard of such things. People who have been through it say that kind is more dangerous and bloodthirsty than Injuns. That's 'cause they got all the cunning and cruelty of white folk, without any restraints of either the red or the white man's way o' livin'."

"How many of you are there?" Stone interrupted to inquire.

"Eighteen, countin' the women and children."

"You'd better start making preparations if you want to ride under our protection to Dodge City."

"How we gonna do that without horses?" the

82

grumpy man who had greeted them so rudely demanded.

"I got a couple of harness teams they didn't run off. Must of figgered plowhorses was too much trouble to feed," Milton Deines offered.

"Well, then," the lieutenant went on briskly, "hitch them to a couple of wagons and load the women and children. Also some food."

"What? Why, that'd leave the men to walk all the way. That'd take a week."

"You cover many a mile a day behind a plow, don't you?" Eli Holten asked coldly, disgusted with this windbag. "Besides, by the route we're going, it'll take the better part of a week to get there anyway."

"It's settled then," the army officer announced. "We'll give you half an hour to make ready."

Four days later, Charlie Roundtree slipped through the back alleys of Dodge City, intently studying the appearance of the strange soldiers, mounted on mules, who were entering town slowly, a buckskin-clad civilian and an officer in the lead, and a bedraggled lot of homesteaders crowded into two sorry-looking wagons behind. He would have to learn more about this. It was obvious that the civilian was a scout. Would he be any good? Charlie wanted to know everything about this newcomer and the odd-looking patrol he scouted for before leaving town. He watched with interest while the soldiers halted near the livery corral and dismounted.

"Sergeant O'Kelly," Lieutenant Stone called. "Make arrangements for quartering the troops on the edge of town. See that the civilians are made comfortable, then dismiss the men. There will be no drinking and no cavorting while we're here. We're close behind these renegades, so we'll be leaving in two hours' time. Now's not a time to lose important miles to a mixed lot of hangovers."

"Yes, sir!"

Stone turned away to speak to Eli Holten when a querulous voice, edged with the bite of a buzz saw interrupted him.

"Would you mind telling me what the Army is doing, languishing in Dodge City, when you should be out there finding the ones responsible for all this turmoil?"

The body that went with the voice was as round as a sawblade, short and squat, with a swelling front, and was tightly encased in a yellow and brown silk vest and a chocolate suit. A derby of the same chocolate color was perched on top of a small, balding head. As to his features, the man so clad could have best been described as a petulant, spoiled cherub. Eyes, set too closely together, seemed to cling to the sides of a long, narrow, disapproving nose that divided his puffy cheeks like the well-honed blade of an axe. His fat, mobile lips—an unnaturally vivid red in so pallid a complexion—pursed into a tight pout of revulsion, as though to gaze upon these representatives of the United States Army was to taste something from the floor of an outhouse. He raised an imperious index finger, curved slightly like the

84

talon of a vulture, and tapped it in Lieutenant Stone's direction by a jerk of his wrist.

"See here, Lieutenant, it ill becomes the reputation of the military for you to be so poorly organized and outfitted as to arrive in our fair city by so ludicrous a means of transportation, utterly unprepared for combat against an enemy, and then simply to remain silent, without any explanation for your dereliction of duty."

The troops had not been dismissed as yet and Sgt. Clerance O'Kelly remained at their front. His face had taken on a beetlike hue and steam threatened to escape through his ears, nostrils, and eyes.

"Why don'cha shove it in yer rear?" O'Kelly snarled *sotto voce*.

"What was that!" the obnoxiously officious civilian thundered in righteous wrath as he rounded on the sergeant.

"I said, 'tis a right honorable career. Providin' ye've the courage to enter it," O'Kelly told him levelly.

For a moment, it appeared as though the tubby townsman would explode from the force of his rising anger. Several of the men closest to him snickered. It only added to his fury.

"I . . . I want that man disciplined, do you hear?"

Richard Stone turned slightly in the saddle. "You're a naughty, naughty boy, O'Kelly," he said with a wicked grin and a wink, neither of which went unnoticed by their tormentor.

"I'll have you know that I am Hiram P. Skaggs,

president of the Farmers' and Stockmen's Trust Bank. Be certain that your insubordinate manner will reach the ears of Colonel Waterstratt. You'll rue the day you crossed me, Lieutenant."

"Oh, yes, sir. Fuck you very much, sir," Stone snapped out at Gatling gun speed, mangling the words so that Skaggs missed their import. Instantly, Holten developed a greater liking for the scar-faced young officer.

"That's better," Skaggs went on, apparently mollified. "Now, I'll ask you once again, what are you doing in town?"

"Escorting civilian survivors of one of those attacks, Mister Skaggs. And following the perpetrators. They are headed northeast and it is our job to encounter them and end their depredations."

"Well . . . Well, then. An admirable task, but shouldn't it be left up to proper cavalry? I mean, after all—"

"Colonel's orders, Mister Skaggs," Eli Holten put in. "He didn't think you civilians would like to wait around until the cavalry could return from patrol along the Colorado border. Or . . . is *that* what you would like to look forward to?" The scout pointed toward the bedraggled collection of survivors.

The wounded, dirty and soot-smelling refugees looked back coldly at the banker. Skaggs lost the last of his pomposity.

"I, ah, that is, er, no. Not at all, naturally. I bid you a good afternoon, Lieutenant. Mustn't interfere with the Army in the commission of its duties, I always say."

After the offensive banker had waddled a block away, Richard Stone let out a prodigious sigh. "That man could have my ass for an umbrella stand, if he wanted. Thanks for your timely assistance, Mister Holten."

"It's Eli, remember, Lieutenant. Now, I'd like a bit of time to tend to Mrs. Walters's needs. I'll join you directly."

"I was sure you would, Eli," the officer returned with a knowing grin. "We'll be down by the cattle pens when you're, ah, finished."

The thickening bulge at Eli's groin had not gone unseen by Stone as the scout took Susan by the hand and led her down the boardwalk toward a likely place to take lodging.

Chapter Seven

"Those jack rabbits them soldier boys is ridin'?" a lounger asked from the doorway to the Varieties saloon, two doors down, his voice a slow, elaborate drawl.

"Naw," an equally scruffy companion responded. "They's jackalopes."

"What's that?" the first demanded.

"A crossbreed of an antelope an' a jackrabbit. They's best for soldiers, 'cause they's even more stupid than those with rides 'em."

That comment brought a round of guffaws from the gathering of idlers who had formed a ring around the unorthodoxly mounted force. The laughter encouraged more insults and Sergeant O'Kelly, himself not noted for his placid temperament, saw clear signs that Lieutenant Stone had endured about all he could take. They could not dismount, as ordered, and lead their beasts away, O'Kelly thought. Honor now demanded that the troops remain astride their lop-eared steeds. He leaned forward, though, and muttered quietly to the young officer.

"Beggin' the lieutenant's pardon, sir. Sure an' the boys is gettin' a wee bit restless. Could be that a short stroll through those bigmouths on the plank walk would loosen up those saddlesore muscles a mite. There ain't but some three to each of our one over there—which by an Army man's lights makes the odds right about even," he concluded, phrasing his last words in the form of a hopeful request.

Lt. Richard Stone sighed resignedly. "Have the men keep their peace *and* their seats, Sergeant. I'm afraid we can't do that, though the prospect does have merit. See that hollow-faced one over there with a mouth like a puckered horse's behind?" Stone went on, massaging the back of one hand with the other. "That jaw of his looks like the right size to fit my knuckles."

O'Kelly whistled tunelessly through his teeth. "By all the Saints, Lieutenant, sure an' it seems like we'll make a reg'lar officer outten ye anyhow, West Point or no West Point."

"Even drummer boys have fist fights, Sergeant O'Kelly. And I was that a long time before Congress made me an officer and a gentleman. No, we'll stand fast until Mister Holten, er, Eli returns."

"What then?"

"He's a civilian. If he finds these insults

unbearable and chooses to do something about it, that can't be helped. Of course, if he does, we would be obligated to go to his aid, since he's also Army property, would we not?"

"Aye, an' that's the truth of it, it is," O'Kelly agreed, a grin spreading over his face. "I like yer way o' figgerin' things, if I may say so, sir."

A familiar figure appeared at the edge of the small crowd. Hiram Skaggs climbed to the bed of a buckboard and raised his hands for order. While the insults still flew through the air, he began to speak to the assembled men.

"Gentlemen . . . gentlemen . . . Come now. There's no cause to linger here and heap abuse upon these fine, brave boys in blue. They are splendid representatives of the United States Army, after all—as are their valiant mounts." That brought a general laugh.

"What? You surely don't feel there is call for levity. Why the officer in charge of this *mulevary* unit assured me they are hot in pursuit of the renegades who have been wreaking destruction on our fair county. Though to fairly examine their manner of doing so, I wonder if those Indian marauders might not be better company?"

"That'll do, Mister Skaggs," Ed Masterson called out in a slow, flat voice. He stood across the street on the boardwalk, arms folded over his vest, disdainfully eyeing the assemblage.

"How's that, Marshal?" Skaggs riposted with a sneer.

"You keep that up and I might have to arrest

you for inciting a riot."

"Now see here. A man's got a right to speak his own mind. Gar'nteed in the Constitution. That's all I was doin'."

"But it don't give him the right to yell 'fire' in a crowded church full of women and children," Masterson threw back. "You fellers move on about your own business before I set O'Brannigan there to bustin' heads." Masterson nodded to the other side of the crowd where Wyatt Earp stood, six-gun in hand and a wicked smile on his lips.

Familiar with the city deputy's penchant for quelling rowdies with a pistol barrel along the side of the head, the idlers muttered among themselves and began to disperse. Both lawmen, and the disgruntled soldiers, watched them coldly as they ambled away.

On a short side street, Eli Holten and Susan Walters paused at the low picket fence before a small, wood-shingled house. A fresh coat of white paint made it glow against the drab surroundings of its neighbors. They had been directed there by the kindly woman who ran a boardinghouse on Cottonwood Street.

"It's only three rooms, but its like heaven to me," Susan breathed out excitedly. "Now that it's mine, at least to rent, let's go in and look it over."

"You'll need a lot of things to make it livable."

"Oh, I'll manage," Susan informed him.

Inside, Susan went about, making little "oohs"

and "aahs" at the chintz curtains, damask drapes, and solid, though somewhat scarred, furniture. In the kitchen she found the cupboards and cabinets bare.

"I'll need pots and pans and dishes. Tableware and, of course, food. But for right now," she added impishly while she crossed the living room to a closed door, "I have everything we need."

She opened the portal with a flourish and revealed a brass bedstead, complete with thick mattress and downy comforters. Quickly, with flying, competent fingers, she began to undress.

"Oh, hurry, Eli. We must . . . must be happy again before you go away with the soldiers."

Holten had no thought of objecting. Already this mighty sword strained at the cloth of his trousers, aching to be freed, only to be once more confined in the sweetest of all prisons.

"How lucky can one man be?" he remarked as he took in each delightful contour of her gleaming terrain. "You have the beauty and endurance of a young girl and the wanton variety of a mature woman. Every time I think of you, I ache with the desire to make love to you."

"Then don't talk, do. Bury yourself deep inside me and I'll take the pain away."

Holten lifted her in his arms and kissed her passionately. Their naked skins grew enchantingly sensitive and volatile shocks of ecstasy raced through their receptive nerve endings. Soon their heads swam in delirium and their hearts pounded with ever-heightening arousal. Mesmerized, Eli stopped kissing the gentle line of her jaw to watch a pulsing blue vein in her throat. He bent forward and brushed the spot with his lips.

As he did, Susan reached downward and began to squeeze and tickle the rigid shaft that pressed against her taut belly.

Slowly she eased it downward until it pressed against the narrow top of her free-flowing cleft. There she worked it around, arousing them further, and fitted it easily into the welcoming canyon beyond. Eli thrust forward from the hips and slid more of his manhood into that tight-fitted sheath. Susan moaned and threw back her head. Eli cupped both hands under her delightfully rounded fanny and she clung to him around the neck. With a rocking motion like posting on a horse, the scout began to propel himself even further into the dark, dripping mysteries of this ever so passionate woman.

Skillfully he worked toward the ultimate, every sense jangled by the perfection of his consummate effort. Then, as tingling sensations gave way to sweet oblivion, he ceased his exertions and bore Susan to the bed.

There he placed her on her back at the very edge, her long, superb legs over his shoulders, while he remained standing and began to undulate in so delightful a manner that they both cried out in incoherent joy as he churned and pounded and worked deeper than ever before into her heated cauldron. Susan dashed her heat from side to side and whimpered on each in stroke as he pierced her to the core of her being. Eli snorted like a rutting stallion and strove to delve even farther up that contracting channel that squeezed like a giant hand, hot and moist and cloying. With a wild shudder, they ascended the final slope, teetered on the brink and plunged into inchoate insensibility.

"You . . . you're too good for me, Eli," Susan panted.

"And I'm also late," the scout returned as she dabbed daintily at his still-distended member, removing the evidence of their amorous struggle. "I'll ask Ed Masterson to give you a hand getting settled in. When this job is done, I'll come back for a while."

"I . . . I can't stand the thought of waiting. I know it sounds trite, but you are definitely the answer to a maiden's prayer. Don't be too long, my darling."

"You didn't get here any too soon," Lieutenant Stone told Eli when he returned to the front of the Long Branch.

"Sorry. I, uh, had to help Susan get settled. There wasn't a place in the boardinghouse."

"We're more than ready to leave." Stone went on to describe the near riot that developed after the scout had left to find Widow Walters a place to lodge.

"Hummm," Eli responded noncommittally. "Seems to be there's a lot more to be found out here. That trail is clear enough to follow for now.

What say I remain behind and pick up what I can about this thing. Knowin' bankers, it seems funny to me that one who could pick up land cheap and sell it dearly later on would be the last one to be raisin' such a fuss about the raids."

"True enough. But he might be hostile to the Army . . . which this Skaggs certainly was. If we stop the scare, he can't buy up cheap land anymore."

"You think he might have some other interest in all this?" Eli asked.

"No." Stone thought a moment. "But what banker wouldn't be quick to take advantage of the situation? He'd naturally resent the loss of his hole card."

"Right enough. Well, I'll dig up what I can and join you sometime late tomorrow. Good luck, Rick."

"You, too, Eli. And don't tarry too long. Your scoutin' ability and knowledge of Indians is sorely needed."

To a scattered chorus of hoots and jeers, the mule-mounted infantry rode, red-faced, out of Dodge. Eli, meanwhile, sought out the best place for a free flow of information—the long, shiny, mahogany bar of the Long Branch. There he received warmer, and less formal greetings from Ed Masterson and Wyatt Earp.

"How'd you get connected up with that, er, odd assortment, Eli?" Masterson inquired.

"It's a long story, Ed. Sometime, when the snows are deep and the women hibernating and

95

the whiskey run dry, I'll tell it to you."

"I gather it's a tale you'd prefer to leave untold," Wyatt suggested.

"Ask the big winner there," Eli replied, hooking a thumb at Masterson. Although reluctant to admit it, he still smarted over his defeat at poker.

"Those clodhoppers you brought in haven't chosen to be any too cooperative," Masterson offered to change the subject. "They're all gathered up down by the cattle pens, moanin' and bitchin' to themselves. I offered to send for Brother Will so's they could give a statement to him, but they said they didn't reckon as how it would do any more good than it has already. What was it you found out, Eli?"

"It looks like these raids are being conducted by half-breeds. Or perhaps some bloods that went renegade after servin' with the Army as scouts. They use bugle calls, fire in unison, charge and volley alternately, and stand in ranks like soldiers."

"That's a lot to swallow," Wyatt remarked through a whistle of doubtful surprise.

"No matter, it's what those pilgrims told us. They wear boots, the sign around the soddies they attacked showed that. Army boots, from the shape of the prints. Lots of expended cartridges. Tell me, Ed, Wyatt, how many times have you seen Indians with enough ammunition—let alone weapons to use it—to leave their brass behind? They always have to reload. And they had plenty of time to gather up most of what they expended out there.

It's been the same at every homestead that has been attacked. Even someone as green as Lieutenant Stone saw that and remarked on it."

"Well . . ." Ed Masterson said cautiously. "If it's really half-breeds involved, I'd be inclined to include that one as a prime suspect." He nodded toward a squat, dark-faced man who stood outside, peering in through the paint-decorated plate-glass window of the saloon.

"That's Charlie Roundtree. He comes by the cavalry pants honestly. Once scouted for General Crook and also for Terry, or so they say. That big black hat's a gift from the Shawnee Mission Indian school he attended. Now he's nothin' but a loafer and a bum. Even so, Charlie never seems to be short of money."

"It's not my business, of course," Eli apologized in advance. "But if that's the case, why do you put up with him bein' in Dodge?"

"He's had a couple of run-ins with Banker Skaggs. Got downright near violent at one point. For that reason, if nothin' else, Wyatt and I tolerate Charlie hangin' around town. It's right pleasant to see someone who can get Hiram Skaggs's goat."

"Way we see it," Wyatt drawled, "Roundtree can't be all bad if Skaggs doesn't like him."

The subject of the conversation—Skaggs, not Charlie—entered the saloon and swaggered to the far end of the high-ceilinged barroom. There he stepped onto the postage stamp stage and made a curt gesture to the piano player to cease his plinking.

"Listen to me!" the banker called out. Slowly the quiet roar of conversation diminished. "Most of you men are residents of Dodge, or live nearby. Some have places out where these renegades have been raisin' hell. Every day we hear more about these depredations. And what does the Army do about it?" Skaggs paused dramatically while he let a sneer twist his face.

"They send us a bunch of foot-sloggin' infantry, mounted on mules. It's time we stop wasting our time expecting the Army to do anything. This latest farce just goes to show that there's not a single soldier in the entire state worth spit. If the men of Kansas, and those of us around Dodge City in particular, are to live free, we must rise up like John Brown and the Jayhawkers and strike down these raiders ourselves."

Scattered cheers and shouts of agreement greeted the banker's inflammatory remarks. He replaced his sneer with a smug smile. Brown-clad arms across his ample belly he seemed to swell, like a horned toad, as the more rowdy element praised this course of action. Then one of the settlers brought in by Stone's patrol stepped forward to protest.

"That's all well an' good, Mister Banker. But how can we go off fightin' the redskins, or whoever they be, if we have to leave our farms and families behind?"

"Why . . . why . . . ?" Skaggs seemed astounded at this line of thinking. "Mister, I don't know who you are, but I do know a lot about this great nation of ours. Traditionally, since the earliest days of the American Revolution, farmers like yourself have willingly, courageously, gone forth from their fields to fight for the common good. It's the least that a man, any *real* man can do."

"It's not the same. What you're talkin' about was fightin' an army of white soldiers, men like ourselves. They didn't threaten the lives and homes of the families of the men who went against them. What we got here, what you ask us to do, is to leave our places open for attack."

"Everyone must make some sacrifices for the common good. You amaze me, sir. Why, if you don't have what it takes to live out here, then . . . the best I suggest is that it might be advisable for you to depart and leave the hard work to others. Much as it offends me, much as I hate to admit it, the bank *is* buying land. If you can't stand the heat, the wise men say, then get out of the furnace." He broke off his preachments to address the other men directly.

"I'll pay this cowardly creature, and any of the rest of you, a fair price for your land. Any man who has proven up on his government claims, yet can't hold it in the face of this small adversity, should sell out and get out. Now there. There's an offer for you."

Red-faced, head bowed and shoulders slumped, the farmer walked closer. "Well now, Mister Skaggs, now that you've put it that way . . . I . . ." He heaved a deep sigh of regret. "Well, damn it all, I reckon I'll be obliged to accept your offer. Why should I be compelled to hang around a town that's got pompous windbags like you, stirrin' a man's blood to folly or gettin' him named a coward before his friends? There's other places out here. I was lookin' when I came, and I can look again. Put up yer money, Banker."

"You're certain? Positive?"

"Damned right I am."

"Well then . . . I . . . I suppose I can accommodate you. I'll pay top dollar, mind. For you and any others. Just step over to that table and bring your deed with you."

"How about me? How about me?" several men chorused. "I'm gettin' fed up, too." Suddenly the tubby little banker found himself surrounded by men with hard, sunburned features, each begging to be next in line to dispose of his hard-won property.

"Settle down, gawdammit!" Ed Masterson bellowed. He slammed an empty whiskey bottle on the bar for emphasis. The sudden uproar subsided gradually. Most of the men turned resentful eyes in his direction.

"Look. There's no reason to lose all hope. Sure, the Army has been slow. First of all they have to be shown, have it proved to them that it is something over which they have jurisdiction. If it's Indians, they go after them. Is that right, Eli?" To the gawking men he made an introduction. "This is Eli Holten, chief scout of the Twelfth Cavalry up in the Dakota Territory. If anyone knows about these things, Eli does."

"That's a lot of praise, Ed. What you said is true,

though. Unless, and until, the Army has solid proof that what is happening is being done by the Indians, or by half-breeds living under government supervision—"

"What's that mean?" an angry voice challenged.

"Mixed-bloods who normally live on a reservation, or among free bands to the west of here. If this is the case, the Army can step in. If not . . . then it is up to the civil authorities. You would have to go to Sheriff Masterson."

"He says it's not his problem. It's Injuns."

"And it may be. We're trying to find out one way or another. If your own sheriff can't or won't do anything, you have to go to Topeka and appeal to the governor."

"Eli's right. There's the state militia and the governor's posse. We're not alone in this. Give the Army some time to look into it. No need to have a run on the bank just yet. If it is white brigands, then we'll send notice to Topeka. The governor will do something for us."

"Yes, friends," Hiram Skaggs said shakily. "That is why I was reluctant to tell you that my bank would buy land. Things aren't all that bad. Not just yet. There's no reason to sell out and run away with your tails between your legs. Think it over. I'm impatient with the Army, true, but that's not cause to turn yellow. Stand fast. Then . . . if things *do* turn worse . . . well, the bank's always here to lend a helping hand." The portly man with the porcine face wiped a chubby hand over his perspiring brow and smiled weakly.

While the landrush-in-reverse was being

quelled, Eli Holten had his eyes fixed elsewhere. With the intensified concentration of the expert hunter who knows he has homed in on an elusive quarry, he watched Charlie Roundtree taking in the show through the front window, avidly focused on it like a vulture waiting for something to die.

Chapter Eight

Besides the rich aromas of turned soil and growing things, the flat, semiarid plains of western Kansas exuded a fine dust. Raw and itchy, and comprised of the pollen of ragweed, goldenrod, and wind-raised silt, it insinuated itself into the nostrils of every man and beast. Along the stretch of the commercial district in Dodge City, horses snorted and stamped, and men hacked, sneezed, and coughed up gobbets of green- and saffron-tinted mucus. The new generation born in this hostile environment, accepted these reactions as natural. To Eli Holten, they were irritating.

Eli had not fully believed Ed Masterson's assurance that any enemy of Hiram Skaggs was a friend of mankind. To his way of thinking, if the raiders were indeed half-breeds, then it would stand to reason that they would have spies in town. Since many mixed-bloods could easily pass as white, their presence would go entirely unnoticed. Accordingly, he set out from the Long Branch to keep Charlie Roundtree under observation.

The trail ended abruptly when Charlie entered the Varieties and, before Holten could follow, disappeared from sight. The scout remained in the saloon for a while, listening to the talk. He made a careful study of the men who were patronizing it, seeking to determine if any of them might be a part of the marauding force. Satisfied with what he saw, he moved on to the Oasis.

All the while he felt as though unseen eyes watched him, but try as he might, Eli could not catch sight of his surveyors. At the Oasis, he ordered a beer and took a long swallow before again beginning his round of questions.

"Have you seen anything of Charlie Round-tree?" he inquired of George, the third Masterson brother, who tended bar at the Oasis.

"Nope. Not since opening today at least. He was here offerin' to carry out the breakage in return for a couple of beers."

"Know him well, George?"

"Naw. Just to see around town. You talked to Ed about him yet?"

"A little while ago, down at the Long Branch."

"Huh. He's a queer duck, you ask me."

"How's that?"

"I've seen trail bosses offer him steady work if he'd ride to Texas with them. Ol' Charlie he would get downright riled by that. No way, he'd say, he would go to Texas. 'Texans hate Injuns,' he'd say. 'Bein' half Injun, I'd have half of me thrown out of every saloon in the state,' he'd go on."

"Can't blame a thirsty man for that," Eli remarked to keep the information flowing.

"There's more'n that, though. Even though we'll serve him in Kansas, I know for a fact he's turned down jobs on farms, ranches, an' for the railroad. Yet, he's never outta money. One of the things he got in a dust-up with Banker Scraggs over was when he paid another man's debt."

"Oh? When did this happen?"

"Uh . . . about six months ago. There was this little farmer—white but he had an Indian wife—got behind in his payments and Skaggs was gonna foreclose. One day Charlie comes ridin' in and pays up the whole shebang. Skaggs was close to foamin' at the mouth. He had his eye on that bit of property, and he'd even taken a downpayment from some folks what wanted it."

"Hummm. Maybe there's something in what Ed says about Charlie being all right if he and Skaggs don't hit it off," Eli speculated aloud.

"Heard you talkin' about Charlie Roundtree," one old-timer remarked from a ways down the mahogany. "George is right. He's a strange one to figger. Claims he's a Ponca breed. Ain't never been many Poncas live around Dodge. Those that have drifted through here never took up with Charlie, nor him with them. Bein' one of their own blood, you'd sort of expect they'd at least swap a few lies together and share a meal. But nope, nary a one."

Eli found he had a small audience now, so he

105

risked throwing out another question to the group. "What about Skaggs? Is he always so sour?"

"You might say that," a well-dressed merchant offered. "At least toward the Army. He never has a good word for the soldier boys. Won't bank their money or forward it to families if they ask him to. Sends them down to the Ark Valley Grange Bank. I've heard of businessmen refusin' to deal with Injuns an' niggers, but never soldiers. Truth to tell, Hiram is a poor banker. He lets his personal feelings influence his business decisions too much. The way I see it, this is a free country. Any man's money spends just as good as the other fellow's. Don't matter to me the color of his skin or who his people are. If someone wants to buy what I've got to sell, I'm willin' to dicker with him."

"You, sir, have the true soul of a Venetian merchant," Eli told him dryly.

The loquacious businessman glowered a second. "Somehow I gather that to have been meant sarcasticlike. But, I take it as a compliment. No, sir. If Hiram Skaggs ran his bank the way I do my mercantile, he'd not be in trouble."

"Oh? What sort of trouble?"

"Not long ago, the major depositors formed a board of trustees. If they pulled their money out, it would start a run and the bank would collapse. So Skaggs had to go along with them. There's a rumor now that Skaggs might be replaced any time by the board. How they figger to do it, I don't know, but that's what's being said."

"Interesting. Would you have any idea what this

board thinks about his offer to buy up land at distress prices because of the raids?"

"Well, ah, no. Not directly. Seems to me, though, that they might get a bit worried. It's their money he's using. If a lot of folks pulled out and no one came in to buy that ground from the bank, it could put a crimp in the works pretty bad. So, I'd guess they would be against it."

"Thank you," Eli concluded. "You've provided a lot of food for thought."

To the east, the day had already died when Eli came out of the Oasis. In the opposite direction, bright blue still held sway and the sun had only begun to make its rapid slide down the last quarter of the sky. He had learned somewhat more than he had set out to discover, though he didn't know if it had any bearing on the main issue. Skaggs was not well liked, and Charlie Roundtree was only tolerated. What did that tell him about the raids?

Nothing, he had to conclude as he strolled along the plank walk. At opposite poles from each other, the two men still seemed equally unconnected to the mysterious renegades who had struck down farm after farm. Yet, Charlie Roundtree had faded out of sight, as though he knew Holten had been following him. The scout pondered that as, up ahead, a disturbance broke out when three drunken men staggered out of a seedy saloon, mouthing profane insults at each other.

Holten drew nearer to them, only to discover what he had sought in the first place. Half-breeds. The trio consisted of dark, squat men with long, black hair and hawk-beak noses. One wore a feather in his tall-crowned, round-topped, ebony reservation hat. The reek of whiskey reached the scout's nostrils before he came within three feet of the reeling, stumbling men. They stopped abruptly and eyed Holten owlishly.

"Him the one?" the breed on Holten's right slurred.

"Unh!" grunted the one in the middle.

Then the three fell on the scout.

Their combined weight and semidrunken state bore Eli down, and before he could react, they had dragged him into a narrow alley between a doctor's office and the funeral parlor. By that time, Eli had managed to land a short, vicious blow under the untalkative one's heart. The man grunted again and went slack, his dead weight hampering the scout's further efforts.

But try, Eli did. He'd managed to draw his Remington and to ear back the hammer when a stout smack from a fire-hardened oak stick numbed his hand. The revolver fell from his nerveless fingers and punches began to land against the scout's rib cage and the sides of his head.

Holten lashed out at his assailants, his fists made ineffective by the confined area and the tight press of their bodies. Even so, he managed to connect with one prominent nose. He heard a satisfying crunch—cartilage—and a torrent of blood began to flow. While still free, he whipped the same closed hand into the side of the bleeding semiconscious half-breed who clung to him.

With a soft moan, the stuporous mixed-blood let go and crumpled to the littered filth that covered the alley floor. Released from one fleshly anchor, the scout managed to pull his Bowie from its sheath and slash the chest of another assailant. A howl of pain rose like a coyote's love call, and a profusely bleeding breed staggered away, clutching at the fire in his savaged muscles. Instantly, Eli leaped to the side and turned on his final tormentor.

A glassy, wide-eyed stare of horror met the scout's icy gaze just before Eli plunged the Bowie to its hilt in the soft stomach of the renegade. With a violent sideways jerk, Holten freed the blade; then hearing a rustle of stealthy footsteps, he whirled.

Two more men came at him. He dodged a swinging war club and the keen edge of his Bowie bit deeply into the thick muscle of the forearm behind the deadly stone weapon. The way to the street should be clear, Eli's mind told him, so he started for it.

Bright lights and explosive pain burst in his head as the broad, flat face of a tomahawk smashed into the back of his skull. Blackness instantly swept over him and he stood, trembling uncontrollably for a brief second before he crashed down into the foul quagmire that covered the alleyway.

Dawn stole across the prairie to the accompaniment of the dolorous melody of mourning doves and the cheerful counterpoint of meadowlarks. A short distance from where the soldiers of Lieutenant Stone's patrol saddled their mules, a mother quail called sharp instructions to her brood of young, mindful of how tasty her kind were considered by skunks, coyotes, and men.

"I've been thinking on it, Sergeant, and I've concluded that we have no other choice. Even though the renegades seem to have disappeared into the grass, we have to continue on north. We'll find sign of them again, I'm sure of that."

"Right ye are, Lieutenant. The boys is rested good and spoilin' to get in shootin' range of these spalpeen bastards."

"Let's hope today's ride gives them that opportunity. I want you, Jensen, and Thomas to ride out as scouts. You have the most experience. With any luck we'll cut their sign within an hour or so."

"As you wish, sir."

Nearly two hours later fresh evidence of the raiders was found when Clerance O'Kelly made a grisly discovery in a gulley carved out by the rushing waters of many past flash floods. He rode back to the column and directed his officer and the troops to the location.

"It's bones, sir. Human bones, I'd say. Of a child at that."

Even the most hardened of the infantrymen cringed at the sight.

"Who . . . who would do a thing like that?" Lieutenant Stone choked out as he gazed upon the blackened and broken bones. Several had what might be teeth marks on them, while others retained scraps of cooked meat.

"Tonkawas, Lieutenant. Ain't no other cannibals around."

"It couldn't be, Sergeant. The Tonks were from south Texas. They were supposed to have been wiped out a long time ago. Even the other tribes joined in on that expedition. We have to look for some other cause."

"Beggin' yer pardon, sir, but I know what it is I'm seein'. Sure an' it's Tonks what done this. I'll stake me stripes on it."

Eli Holten awoke with a start. Slowly, as his awareness increased, he recognized the rough, rolling moiton of a wagon and felt the tight bindings that held him captive. After listening intently for several moments, he slowly cracked open his eyes.

Bright sunlight poured down into the open bed of the buckboard, turning his throbbing head into an active hive of vengeful wasps. Agony made him nauseous, and he swallowed rapidly to contain the bitter bile rising in his throat. Gradually, Holten's swimming vision cleared and he saw the dark, hunched form of the man on the driver's seat. Eli made an involuntary grunt when the off wheel struck an especially deep rut and the figure moved.

Charlie Roundtree turned to look over his shoulder at the prisoner. "You have come awake, I see."

"Sort of. What do you intend to do with me?"

"Curious, are you? I'll try to inform you. Since you have taken such an interest in me, I thought the least I could do was see we got better acquainted."

Holten replied with a grunt, followed by a question. "Where are we?"

"Southeast of Dodge City. We're on the way to where I live. You'll like it, I'm sure. It's along the north bank of the Arkansas River. Lots of trees, it's cool in summer, sheltered in winter. I have sixty men gathered there. It's sort of our permanent camp."

Holten registered his surprise at this frank revelation by raising his eyebrows. "Those have to be the renegades who've been attacking home-steads around here. Why are you telling me all of this?"

"Oh, I have nothing to hide. You see, Mister Scout Eli Holten, you'll never come out of this alive. I'm sure you knew that when you woke up tied like the pig you are."

"Ah . . . what makes me so important that you single me out for special attention?"

Charlie released a short, sharp bark of laughter. "You see, with a single stroke I have taken out the only man in the area who can scout well enough, and figure things out accurately enough, to lead those mule-humping soldiers anywhere near my hiding place; or to figure out where I might strike next. I came to that conclusion when you expressed too much curiosity about me in Dodge City."

"Wasn't that a bit of a risk? I mean, taking me off the streets of Dodge like that?"

"Not at all. Those fools!" Charlie reveled. "They think of me as Poor Charlie. The dumb half-breed. Lazy, that's what Charlie is to them.

Well, I'm showing them. I'll show all you whites."

"You're part white, too, Charlie."

"Not so's you'd notice. At least the *inside* part of me is Indian. And that part, Mister Scout, that part will not rest until the whites are run out of Kansas."

As though he had said, entirely too much, Charlie Roundtree broke off and remained stubbornly silent for the next ten body-bruising miles. Although Holten tried to coax him into conversation, the half-breed would only hunch his shoulders tighter and grunt a noncommittal reply. By noon the horses had become heavily lathered from the exertion of pulling the unsprung wagon and its contents of flour, sugar, coffee, and the scout. Shortly after midday, Holten's nostrils began to tingle to the cooler, moist scent of air that has traveled over water.

Unable to rise, he could rely only on this source of information to tell him that the wide, sandy-bottomed Arkansas River lay not too far away. Half an hour passed, by his estimate, before he saw the tall tops of ancient cottonwoods swaying in the pale blue arc of sky that comprised his entire view outside the wagon. Over the rumble of the wheels, his keen ears picked up the sound of voices and the whickering of pastured horses.

"We're here." Charlie sparingly notified the scout after he pulled the team to a halt.

A quick slash of restraining cords, then rough hands set the scout upright.

He saw an almost unbelievable sight. The wagon had brought him into a small village of stunted lodges. Some were the traditional buffalo-hide dwellings of the plains tribes; others were shanties made of cut brush that was plaited in layers to form a windbreak and to provide at least partial shelter from rain. A few canvas tents, including two large Army Sibleys, rounded out the mismatched village.

The men who inhabited this strange community on a grassy shelf in a wide, sheltered bend of the river were all half-breeds. Holten saw that at once. Here and there he noticed the skirts of a woman or a partially matured girl. English was the prevailing language the scout heard, though smatterings of several tribal tongues filtered through too. Several of the inhabitants looked up at Charlie's arrival.

Quickly they spread the word of the presence of a white captive. Angry mutters turned to shouted insults and a crowd quickly formed. One skinny, pimple-faced half-breed hurled a fresh, wet horse turd that splashed liquidly against Holten's chest. Hoots of approval rose from the onlookers. Charlie grabbed his prisoner by the collar and yanked him over the side of the wagon.

Lancing pain ran over the scout's side as rough splinters gouged into his flesh. Stoically he kept his face expressionless, grateful for the knowledge of self-control he had gained through years of living with the Sioux. Charlie and another mixed-blood frog-marched the scout to a low scaffold where they quickly bound their captive to the accompaniment of yells of approval. Then, before

114

the howling mob could fall upon its prey, Charlie leaped onto the wagon and raised his arms for attention.

"Brothers!" he shouted, then waited while the cries dwindled slightly. "Brothers, at-*tention*!" he bellowed.

Taking his clue, the renegade bugler tooted the brief notes of the command.

Satisfied, Charlie went on in a quieter voice. "Before we test the courage of this white pig, there is food to distribute. Before we watch them bleed and suffer, let me tell you of the money we will make. When I went to Dodge City to get these supplies, I learned that the whites are begging to sell their land. Soon . . . soon now we will be rewarded."

He went on to appeal to the greed in their white natures and the lust for glory and *coups* in their Indian inheritance. His hypnotic voice droned on, searching out the strengths and weaknesses of his followers like a general probing the picket lines of his enemy. Spared for the moment from the torments to come, Holten had a chance to recognize the strange nature of the relationship Roundtree shared with these other half-breeds. Through it all, he began to realize that this charismatic leader was not being entirely up front with his followers.

Roundtree's promise of something to be shared mutually in the future held little substance, the scout believed. The paltry valuables the raiders stole from the soddies would hardly recompense them for the risks they took. Surely those would not satisfy a man like Charlie Roundtree. The scout began to wonder what else the renegade leader was getting out of all this. At last the harangue ended and Charlie crossed over to Holten to begin a test of the scout's mettle.

Chapter Nine

Candlelight flickered in a yellow circle on the creamy linen tablecloth and the white-coated Delmonico's waiter whisked away the soup bowls without a single clatter. Susan Walters sat in a plush, round-backed chair across from the short, dumpy figure of Hiram Skaggs. She had responded to his dinner invitation because of the other offer that had been attached to it. So far, that subject had not come up.

"Well," Skaggs said primly, "while we wait for the entree—and you'll love the stuffed quail, my dear—I suppose we should discuss the purpose of this festive occasion. You are, I believe, looking for employment? How are you with figures?"

"Why, I . . . I know my sums well enough. I can divide and multiply. And I have a neat hand,

Mister Skaggs.''

Skaggs reached a pudgy hand across the table to affectionately pat Susan's nervous one. "I'm sure you do. But I had to ask. Such things are important in the banking business. Have you ever used a ledger book?''

"No. I've seen them. A person puts figures in columns and they are supposed to balance out at the bottom of the page, isn't that so?''

The portly banker clapped his hands in delight. "That's exactly it. And . . . please, call me Hiram.''

"This is . . . leading us somewhere, ah, Hiram?''

"It is, Susan. Let me assure you. There will be a vacancy at the bank come next Monday. Willard Hankins is leaving for another post in Wichita. So far I have relied on exclusively male employees. Now I feel it is time for a change. To be more, ah, modern. Besides, your lovely face and engaging smile would be an asset to the bank. Mind you, this is a clerking job. You would not be in a teller's cage, subjected to the leers of some of our rougher clientele, or the possible danger of a holdup man.''

For a moment, Susan's eyes left the pudgy face of the man across from her and focused on distant space. Pointed thoughts crossed her mind. After all, she needed to fend for herself now. That meant taking some sort of employment. Her family had moved on to California, believing they had left her in the hands of a good husband and provider. Even were she to join them, that would take money, which she presently lacked to an embarrassing extent. The job in the bank sounded promising.

"As to the pay, it shall be generous. Though, of

course, since you are not a man, with a family to support, it would be lower than such a person would earn. You understand that, don't you, Susan?''

"Uh . . . y-yes. It . . . seems that's the way it is everywhere. I know for certain that a man clerking in the general mercantile earns eight dollars a week. I was offered the same position at five, though it seems hardly fair.''

Skaggs uttered a brief, unpleasant chuckle. "It's a man's world, Susan. We must all learn to live in it. Of course,'' he added with a hungry leer that had nothing to do with the savory plate of heavily sauced venison steak the waiter placed before him, "there are other considerations which, if properly and diligently pursued, could earn you rapid promotion and, naturally, increases in salary.''

Susan blinked. She had a notion where this conversation might be leading and that suspicion did little to reassure her. "I don't think I understand you, ah, Hiram.''

"Oh, surely you do. It's the way business is done. Greater effort receives higher reward. Am I being sufficiently specific now?'' His hand darted out to insistently squeeze Susan's.

Oh, yes, quite specific, Susan thought with a slight shudder. According to her observations, Skaggs was a disagreeable person at best. How the fat little man, who sweated too freely, might be as an employer she had no way of knowing. As a possible suitor, or a lover . . . well, her stomach turned at the mere suggestion of that.

"I'm not trying to pressure you, dear Susan.

119

Take your time in considering the, ah, offer. It could only be to your advantage. Give me your answer tomorrow, or the next day. Even Saturday would do. We're open until noon on Saturday, you know. Ah! Here comes your quail. Enjoy it, my dear.''

This may be your last meal. Susan completed the sentence in her mind. Yet, she realized the banking job had its advantages. She had hoped for something with fewer strings—at least less obvious ones—attached, or much more palatable emotional involvement.

As though reading her thoughts, Skaggs remarked casually, through a mouthful of venison which he chewed vigorously, ''Don't count on any help from your friend, Mister Holten. The Army is made up of riffraff and ne'er-do-wells. Your scout can hardly be different. I can deliver, Susan. You may never see Holten again. It's just the nature of the beast. Do let me know tomorrow, if you can . . . will you?''

Her appetite spoiled, Susan mechanically worked her way through the rest of the meal. Skaggs walked her to the picket fence outside her small, rented home and she entered hurriedly, protesting a sudden headache.

There she undressed and flung herself across the bed. It took a long time to cry herself to sleep.

''I'm gettin' worried, Lieutenant.''

''How's that Sergeant O'Kelly?'' Lt. Richard Stone inquired.

"Well, sir," the sergeant replied as he stood to replenish his coffee. "It's about Mister Holten. He said he would catch up with us sometime today."

"Or tomorrow. Don't forget that."

O'Kelly gazed intently into the flickering embers of the evening campfire, averting any contact with his superior's eyes. "Beggin' the lieutenant's pardon, sir," he began with a formality that Stone recognized as a preamble to criticism of his own conduct. "No disrespect meant, sir, but it's sorta stupid for us to be wanderin' out here without some expert tracker to guide the way. We've done lost them renegades again. Sure an' we'd be a sorry sight if they was to slip around behind us and attack, now wouldn't we?"

Stone smiled tolerantly. "I'll concede that last, Sergeant. As to the foolhardiness of our 'wandering' around out here, as you put it, without a scout, I'd remind you that it is our job to do so. If soldiers of the United States Army weren't considered competent enough to perform all necessary duties something would have been done about that, don't you think?"

"Yes, sir. An' that's the truth of it."

"Well then, there is no provision on the TO and E for assigned scouts. It would appear the high command considers us able to do that task for ourselves."

"Beggin' yer pardon again, sir. But out here on the frontier, all them fine theories go up in a puff o' smoke, sir. We ain't lookin' for a bunch o' soldiers who are out here lookin' for us to fight a formal battle. Whether it's half-breeds, like Mister

Holten thinks, or Injuns, or the Lord knows what, these fellers know how to cover their trail. They fight like soldiers, but they ain't in no hurry for a pitched battle. In that, they think like Injuns. Sure, the darlin' little monsters—whatever they might be—are entirely capable of slidin' around our flank and hittin' us in the rear. To find out if that's what's in the works, we need a scout. From what I've seen of him, Mister Holten is one of the best."

Stone scowled a moment, arm extended with his empty cup for the sergeant to refill. In the near distance, the men talked in low voices—mostly, Stone reflected, about their aches and pains from hours of mule-back travel, with a few choice words thrown in about the poor rations for field service and the lack of the wheeled vehicles that customarily accompanied a column of infantry or cavalry to transport some of the amenities of garrison life. So far, their situation was far from untenable. Even so, O'Kelly had made a telling point.

"What do you propose, Sergeant?"

"Officers propose, sir," O'Kelly replied, paraphrasing a familiar attribute usually ascribed to God. "Noncoms dispose."

"Well, then . . . I suggest we send a three-man detail back along our trail to make contact with the scout."

"All the way to Dodge City, sir?"

"If need be."

O'Kelly smiled, greatly relieved. "Sure, an' them's orders that makes music to me ears, sir. I'll

122

attend to it at once."

By the time darkness had slid down to the western horizon, Charlie Roundtree had used several brutal tortures on Eli Holten. One such had consisted of thrusting dried strips of cottonwood bark under the scout's fingernails and lighting them, one by one, with a flaming brand.

Though Eli's muscles contracted involuntarily at the pain, he remained silent, his face frozen in a blank expression. For a long while afterward, the stench of burned human flesh hung heavily in the air.

When arrows, driven by hand through the loose flesh of Holten's upper shoulders, chest, and throat, had failed to elicit a single scream or grunt, Charlie signaled for a halt. He walked close to the dangling captive and spoke in a quiet voice.

"You do well for a pig of a white man."

Holten looked up at him and smiled contemptuously. "I am not entirely white. In the land of the sacred Black Hills, I am known as Tall Bear of the Oglala, a Sioux warrior by full rites and *hunkapi* of Bear Claw's entire band." The scout had spoken in a loud, strong voice and used the Dakota word that indicated relationship to everyone in a village.

It drew some mutters of consternation from the few who had a familiarity with the language. Charlie Roundtree widened his eyes in shocked discovery. Before he could recover, Holten went on.

"You have yet to find anything that will test the courage of a Dakota warrior. I endured greater pain as a boy in the sacred Sun Dance. *Maka kin le, mitawa ca!* I own the earth!" he repeated in English for those who did not understand.

Superstitious dread clutched at Charlie's suddenly pounding heart. This scout, Holten, had powerful medicine. He dare not kill this white Sioux until he could successfully break the man. Charlie's eyes shifted their gaze from the fettered scout to his followers and back. He had to constantly prove that his medicine was the most powerful. Now Holten had given him a bad turn. Perhaps some among the surly mixed-bloods would think the booty they gathered and the promise of a share in land sales was not enough. He would have to do something . . . and fast.

"Cut him down. Take the scout to my biggest lodge. Spread him out and make sure the bonds are tight."

"Why?" "Let's kill him now!" Shouts rose from the gathered renegades.

"No!" Charlie barked in desperation. "His . . . I . . . My medicine says that we are to reserve this one for a special ritual. I . . . I will be shown in a dream how he is to die. Then, after we have completed our most ambitious raids, on which we ride tomorrow and for days to come against the towns of the white men—against Cimarron and Haggard—then we will celebrate our mightiest victory to the music of Holten's screams! I have said this. This we will do! Gather your weapons. Load them well. Make ready the horses and provisions for the trail. We ride before dawn!"

"Lieutenant, we ain't found a horse turd nor a hoofprint," Clerance O'Kelly dejectedly told Lieutenant Stone at the noon meal break the next day.

"Which tells us what, Sergeant O'Kelly?"

"Them renegades ain't givin' us the slip, sir. They ain't here at all."

"Explain that for a slow-witted West Pointer, Sergeant."

O'Kelly grinned. The longer this patrol stayed out, the better he began to like Stone. "Well, sir. What I'm gettin' at is that we're not findin' tracks because any that was laid down is so old now that weather and critters have wiped them out. The raiders has gone to roost wherever it is they hang out between bouts of attackin' the homesteads."

"Then we'd be just as well off if we followed that detail back to Dodge City. If we pressed hard we could make it by late this evening."

"If them's yer orders, sir . . ."

"They are, Sergeant. After the men finish eating, load everything and we'll head back to Dodge at forced march. Something tells me we'll have a better chance of hearing about the renegades there."

"Look there!" Hiram Skaggs shouted to the other men on the oil-lamp-lighted street in front of the Long Branch. "Look at our mighty soldiers comin' back here with their tails between their legs and heads hanging. An inspiring sight, is it not?"

Lieutenant Stone led his exhausted detail down the darkened main thoroughfare of Dodge City, he and his men feeling every bit as dejected as they'd been said to be by the offensive banker. He paid no attention to the yammerings of their leather-lunged detractor. Darkness had caught them still six miles from town and their progress had slowed to a fraction of their former pace. Now, at ten o'clock, all the young officer wanted was a bed, a bath, and a bottle . . . in any order in which they came. Where was Holten, though?

A man in uniform stepped off the boardwalk and delivered a snappy salute.

"Private Compton, sir. The detail regrets to report that there is no sign of Mister Holten and no one in town seems to know where he went."

Damn, he'd quit asking nagging questions of himself if the answers kept coming like that, Stone reflected, disappointed with the news. "Very well, Private Compton. Have accommodations been acquired for the detail?"

"Yes, sir. Corporal Hastings saw to it when we didn't have time to head back today, sir. We're down by the cattle pens."

"Remarkable. A town this size and three men can't find civilized beds when they need them."

"The, ah, only place with rooms has a new sign, sir. It reads No Horses, Dogs or Soldiers. I, ah, thought you'd want to know that, sir."

"Thank you, Private. It saves the embarrassment of asking on my own." Another night on the ground, Stone grumbled to himself. So much for the bed and bath. He'd settle for the bottle.

"What are you doing back here, Lieutenant?" Hiram Skaggs inquired nastily as he walked up to where the detachment had halted. "Hiding in Dodge City won't stop the raiders from killing innocent men and women out on the prairie, now will it?"

Tiredly, Stone answered the banker. "They aren't out there anymore, Mister Skaggs. They've gone to ground somewhere."

"A fine state of affairs," Skaggs continued as though he had not heard the officer's remark. "The Army has plenty of guards for their own supply wagons, but nothing for the poor, honest farmers on their homesteads. Mark my words, if these idlers don't do their job, and soon, we're in for a terrible blood letting. A regular massacre."

The abuse had become too much to endure, so although mindful of how it would appear in his efficiency report, Stone nevertheless gave vent to his anger. "Mister Skaggs, were I you, I'd take extra special precaution that you don't become the first victim of that massacre . . . by the Army, not the renegades. If you haven't anything better to do than open that snotty little mouth of yours and puke up bullshit, I'd suggest you go home and sleep off that drunk."

"Why . . . ! You . . . you impudent puppy! You'll live to regret those words."

"Sure an' you needn't be dirtyin' yerself with the

127

likes o' him, Lieutenant," Clerance O'Kelly's voice boomed out. "By yer leave, sir, an' let me step down an' kick his greasy ass up betwixt his lard-covered shoulder blades."

"I'm tempted, Sergeant. But for now, let's go bed down the men."

Chapter Ten

By the time Richard Stone had come back uptown to purchase a bottle, Hiram Skaggs had taken his customary seat at a table near the rear of the Long Branch. Stone entered, took note of the obnoxious banker and walked to the bar. On impulse, he ordered a double shot and stood watching the wily financier operate.

A desperate-looking sodbuster angled up to Skaggs. The dark circles under his eyes indicated that he had not slept well in some time and had been getting considerable pressure at home. The scared settler stood with his hat clutched in both hands and spoke quietly to the banker.

"Mister Skaggs. I, uh, you were talkin' the other day about buyin' our land at top dollar. Well, I've proved up. Got my deed right here with me. The place is free an' clear. Is it . . . is it true that you'll pay me fair market on it?"

Sadly, Skaggs shook his head. He frowned at the nervous farmer. "The Board of Trustees has ordered the bank not to offer to buy any more property. I'm sorry. I can do nothing about it. They say we can no longer take the long-term risk of buying at market price."

"But . . . but . . ." the crestfallen homesteader protested weakly. "That land is all I've got. I'll have to make a new start somewhere. Yet, my wife an' children have to come first. I've been hearin' about these raids . . . and what you've been sayin' about the Army. If it's as bad as you picture it, it would be best to cut my losses and leave Kansas."

"I can understand that. And I wish I could do something for you. But, just as the trustees won't let me pay you a fair price for your property, there's no one who would give the bank market value either. Not with all this murderin' and destruction going on. If only . . . if only you could hold on." The banker paused to seemingly screw up his strength. "I honestly believe that things will get better someday. Maybe not this month, maybe not this year, or the year after that. But it will happen."

"I can't wait that long, Mister Skaggs. My family . . . I mean, we gotta be able to live without always lookin' over our backs for some murderin' savages to come howlin' down on us. We got a right to that, don't we?"

Skaggs sighed heavily. "Honestly, I believe you do. I sympathize, I really do. I'll tell you what. I'll give you the best offer the trustees have authorized me to make. Trust me, it's the best deal you'll find right now for your property. Ten cents on the dollar."

Crushed, the settler seemed to sag and become diminished as he stared incredulously at the greedy leer of the fat banker. Such an offer would leave him without almost nothing. Not a dime to show for the years of hard, back-breaking work. Tears filled the stricken man's eyes. At the bar, Lieutenant Stone took this scene in and it slowly fed the banked fires of his anger toward Skaggs.

"But . . . that would wipe me out!" the farmer protested when he finally found his voice.

"No one else is buying," the banker countered. "It's the best deal I can make. It's take it or leave it, I'm afraid."

Broken, the homesteader dropped into a chair and produced his deed. With a shaky, reluctant hand he signed in the proper places and relinquished his claim in favor of the bank. Behind a mask of sorrowful compassion, Hiram Skaggs gloated over his success. The tenth such clandestine sale he had made in the last two days.

It might be a little risky, he thought, using the bank's money and placing the property in his own name, but it was worth it. At least he stood to make a huge profit from the temporary distress of the farmers. Flock of fools. Expect the Army to do something. How?

In light of everything he knew, Hiram Skaggs really wondered how the Army—or anyone—could act in time to prevent a mass exodus from all of western Kansas.

Susan's heart lifted at the sound of the late-night knock. It had to be Eli. He had finished his assignment and come back to her. Her feet moved speedily to open the door for him.

"Good evening, Susan," Hiram Skaggs said in syrupy tones, a lascivious grin on his face. He stood on the small stoop, a few scraggly flowers in one hand, his derby hat in the other.

Arctic ice coated Susan's reply. "What are you doing here, *Mister* Skaggs?"

"Please. Remember, it's 'Hiram' and 'Susan,' eh?"

"I'm afraid not, Mister Skaggs."

"I called . . . to discuss my offer again. I'd heard nothing today, so I thought we could get together . . . sort of share a bit of ourselves and that way get to know each other better." He pressed forward, in an attempt to force his way through the door and past her tautly resisting body.

"Sorry. I don't believe that the banking position is right for me."

"Oh, but let me persuade you otherwise," Skaggs purred as he came forward another step until he nearly touched her.

"Mister Skaggs! If you please!" Susan blurted out, shocked and unable to think of effective words to say. She could read the expectancy of imminent compromise in his glowing eyes.

"Top o' the evenin' to ye, Miz Walters," a usually friendly voice that now rumbled with implied menace called from the little gate in the picket fence.

"Why, good evening, Sergeant O'Kelly," Susan responded in a flood of relief. "What . . . what brings you over this way?"

"I was only meanin' to call on ye for a short while. It's about Mister Holten it is."

"The lady is otherwise occupied, can't you see that you lout?" Skaggs growled.

"Na' I don't think that's quite the right o' it, you ask me," O'Kelly riposted in a light tone.

"Why, you bog-trotting ignoramus, get away from here before I have you hauled in for misconduct with a lady."

"Would ye be willin' to step down close here an' repeat that, ye overstuffed piece of horse dung?"

Skaggs hurled down the limp offering of flowers and started toward the dark silhouette of the sergeant. "By God, I will!"

He got within arm's reach. Then O'Kelly flattened the fuming banker with a hard left and a mean right cross.

"Bravo, Sergeant!" Susan cheered from the stoop. "Won't you please come in? I . . . I'm so worried about Eli."

"Are ye now?" O'Kelly asked amiably as he came closer. "An' why would that be?"

"Isn't he with you?"

"Why, no, mum. I came by to inquire what ye might know of him."

Dread, deep and hollow, emptied Susan of all happiness. "But I thought . . . He has been gone since the same night you rode out of town. I

133

thought naturally, that he'd learned what he wanted to know and had ridden to join you."

"No. Now then, let's not be for worryin' over much about Mister Holten. He can take care of hisself, he can. What about this sorry excuse of a man layin' out yonder there? Has he been, ah, out of line, so's to speak?"

"More than that, Sergeant O'Kelly." Susan sighed deeply. Her hands were white so tightly was she clenching them. She took a deep breath and explained everything to O'Kelly. At the end of her narrative, the Irishman fumed with righteous fury.

"I shoulda made a finish of him, I should. You'll not be wantin' to stay close about the likes o' that. But where?" O'Kelly brightened. "We've some, ah, lookin' around yet to do. So we won't be goin' back to the fort. But there's a supply wagon in that'll be headin' out tomorra with the dawn. Could ye be ready to ride along?"

"Oh, yes. Yes, Sergeant."

"Foine, then. When ye get there, go to Mrs. Waterstratt. Her old man's a grouch and a cross far all good soldiers to bear, bein' he's the commandin' officer, but she's a dear. Tell her of yer troubles with Mister Smartpants Banker Skaggs an' she'll see yer provided for."

"Oh, bless you, Sergeant O'Kelly."

"My pleasure, mum," O'Kelly replied through a furious blush.

"And . . . if it happens Eli is there, I'll prevail on him to rejoin your platoon."

O'Kelly had to smile at the improbability of

that. Even so, he definitely had Eli Holten on his mind when he left the widow's residence and swaggered uptown to the Long Branch.

It didn't take long for O'Kelly to find out that, when last seen, Eli had been asking questions about a half-breed known as Charlie Roundtree and that no one had seen Roundtree around town since Holten had disappeared.

Eli tried his best to ignore the pain that tore at his body with incandescent claws. But as he lay in the dark, small insects added to his torment. Mosquito bites raised welts on his face and the tender parts of his groin. Ants and other unseen creatures feasted on or befouled his wounds. Outside the skin lodge, a babble of voices announced hurried preparations for yet another foray by the half-breed army of Charlie Roundtree. Bugle calls accompanied the activity. They were somewhat slurred and off-key due to the drunken state of the bugler. When at last "Assembly" had been blown and the whole horde had ridden out with wild whoops and screeches, and the last mongrel dog had yapped its farewell, silence came to the camp.

The quiet brought no peace or rest to the scout. Sleepless, helpless to combat the swarms of insects, he lay in silent torment as time inched by. A scraping noise at the back of the lodge made him tense. Had Charlie somehow managed to slip away from his followers and come back to kill him? Or had he sent another to do his bidding?

A swift, darting motion convinced him it had to be one or the other. Then a figure resolved itself close at hand.

A half-starved, mad-looking young woman came stealthily to where the scout lay. Spittal dribbled from the corner of her mouth and filth encrusted her to such an extent that it was impossible in the darkness to determine her color or even her features beyond a blunt nose. She knelt and reached out a timid hand to touch his face.

When he moved slightly, she instantly recoiled. "Oh!"

"Who are you?" Holten whispered, the effort it took to form the words nearly sapping him of consciousness.

"I . . . I don't remember. N-no. I'm . . . I'm Al . . . Alicia."

"How long have you been here, Alicia?" the scout asked, impatient to get to more important things, like getting freed.

"I . . . don't know. It's almost summer, isn't it? It was summer when I came here. . . ." Her voice drifted off.

At least a year, the scout thought. "Listen to me, Alicia. Can you get a knife? Cut me loose?"

"Y-yes. I . . . have one here. I . . . I'll help you escape if you will take me along."

"Of course I'll take you. I couldn't leave you here, could I?"

"Oh, good. I gathered up all of your things, even brought your horse."

At closer examination, Holten realized the half-crazed young woman could hardly be eighteen. He strained against his bonds, wondering why she had not already released him.

"That's good, Alicia," Holten whispered, forcing himself to be calm and patient. "Now cut the ropes."

"I will . . . if . . . you see, I want more than to be taken away."

"What do you mean?"

Madness tainted her words as she began to describe in explicit language what he must do, and in which orifices, to ensure her cooperation. "I . . . saw this," she cooed as she reached out and tweaked his flaccid manhood. "I saw how long and pretty it was. I want it. I want to lick it and suck it and roll it between my tits. Oh, it's the biggest I ever saw."

Struck by her coarse, direct manner of speech, stupefied to hear what was coming from this demented thing, Eli could only stare at her in the feeble light. She would be pretty enough, if clean. But she was so thin and fragile.

"Yes, Alicia, yes. Cut me loose and we'll talk about it."

"Oh, no. I want to be sure. I . . . before I came here I was with Alva Elkhorn and some breeds for five years, down on the Washita. He taught me everything. And now I want to do it all with you."

"Cut me loose. It's nearly daylight. We'll never get out of here if we don't go now."

"I will," Alicia murmured, her powerful seizure apparently diminished for a short while. "I will.

Right after I . . ."

"Alicia!" Holten protested in a strangled shout as she bent over his partly responding organ.

"You're no fun," she pouted.

Then his bonds came loose with tiny snaps as the knife in her hand bit through the ropes.

Chapter Eleven

Cimarron constituted little more than a pimple on the prairie. Seen from a distance, its skyline consisted of a low church steeple, the peaked roofs of a dozen one- and two-story houses, a three-story, tin-covered grain elevator and storage silo, and a scattering of outhouses. As elsewhere in blustery Kansas, what few trees existed had been given a permanent northeasterly slant by the strong, prevailing winds. While the mighty, disciplined horde of renegade half-breeds waited behind a rolling swale, out of sight of the small farming community, Charlie Roundtree and five of his men divided into pairs and prepared to ride boldly on the town from different directions.

"The saloon is small," Charlie advised his scouting party. "But notice that it is well stocked.

There is no bank. Money is deposited at the general store until it can be sent to Dodge City to be banked there. You two make a special study of the mercantile. Find it's weaknesses. See if the big safe in the back is open or locked. You, Gray Duck, are to count the number of men in town, on the street and in the shops. Especially the ones with guns. While he does that, Joe," Charlie told his most trusted lieutenant, "you check on the feed and grain place. Many men loaf there when their farmwork is light. They play cards and talk about their troubles. Some have a shotgun or rifle with them. Make a count of these. Big Nose Waller will come with me. We will look over the other stores in town." He studied the expressionless features before him and forced a smile.

"Don't forget to tally the number of comely white women and girls in town. Our brothers will want to know about that, eh?" These remarks provoked wicked chuckles, and Charlie relaxed, knowing he had broken their tension. It would not do, he knew, for them to go into town acting furtive or jumping at the least surprising noise or question. "Act naturally. You are in town to idle away a day, to drink a few beers, and maybe drum up a horse race. Be yourselves, only keep constantly on the watch. Let's go now."

They split and, in pairs, rode into Cimarron.

Dawn had already spread a blue-white glow over the horizon when Eli Holten, leading Sonny and Alicia slipped among the cottonwoods and around the eastern bank of the campsite. The girl had chosen wisely, the scout decided when he saw the rangy mustang she had selected for her own mount. Despite her maddening preoccupation with sex, she had properly saddled the horses and had tied down the few supplies she'd deemed necessary. At least they each had two canteens. Once beyond earshot of the camp, they paused.

"You are sure there are only a few young men guarding the place?" Eli inquired.

"Oh, yes. Mostly boys. Some even too young to be given guns."

"I'd judge we've given them the slip for now. We'd better be moving on."

"Anything you say, Eli," she panted. "But, first, don't you want—"

"No! I don't want anything." Eli paused at the hurt look in the girl's eyes and relented slightly, if only for kindness' sake. "At least until we're well away from here."

Alicia smiled brightly. "All right then, just so long as you keep our bargain."

Unseen by the girl, Eli shuddered at the prospect.

Unseen by both of them, a youth about fourteen years old entered the large tipi where the captive scout was kept. His eyes widened in surprise when he saw the empty space, the severed bonds, and the tracks that led to the rear of the lodge, where the skirt had been pulled upward. Already wise in the ways of this new sort of war, he did not let out a cry of rage or alarm.

Instead, he went quietly from one to another of

his comrades and told them of the escape. A quick search of the camp elicited the fact that the captive slave, Alicia, had also departed.

"This is a bad thing," the young half-breed told his companions. "If Charlie Roundtree comes back and finds them gone, we will be shamed. Worse, we will be punished. We must go after them, look for tracks, find which way they go. Some of us will stay to guard the camp, the others will come with me to run down the scout and the slave with him."

Separated from his visitor by the broad expanse of his dark wooden desk, Hiram Skaggs glowered at the man. He had come down early to work on his private accounts, the ones that involved transactions with the frightened homesteaders who had eagerly sold him their land at a dime on the dollar. Fools, he thought again as he waited for the man to complete his report. They should know that this thing could not go on forever. Before long the Army would come down in force on the renegades and kill them off or run them out of the area. In the meantime, however, he would have made a tidy profit on these deals—depending, of course, on whether or not the trustees discovered his appropriation of bank funds to make the purchases. Thoughts of that possibility and of the yawning gates of a prison sent a shudder up his spine.

". . . O'Kelly . . ."

Mention of that name brought sharper attention

from the banker. It also sent a twinge of pain radiating from his jaw. He had used a tinted salve to cover the bruises, but invisible or not, they still hurt. Also, three teeth wobbled loosely in their sockets. He would get even with this O'Kelly. Of that he was certain. A little social call on the commandant at Fort Dodge should see the loutish Irishman cut down to private again, if not flogged. No, Skaggs remembered with regret, the Army had quit using flogging as a punishment.

Not soon enough, however, to prevent the ugly purple-red welts that crisscrossed his back. Recollection of the pain and humiliation that had accompanied the execution of his sentence sent a tide of rage washing through Skaggs's veins. Stripped of his gold epaulettes with the twin silver bars, the buttons cut from his tunic, his body laid bare to the waist and tied to a post, he had been whipped like a dog. That flogging had left indelible scars not only on his back but on his soul. The final indignity of being frog-marched off the grounds of the fort to the slow beat of drums had been nothing to the pain and horror of what had gone before.

Capt. Hiram Skaggs of the Union Army no longer existed. In his place there lived only a shrunken and defeated man. Branded a coward and publicly disgraced, he had found every man's back turned to him. He could obtain neither lodging nor work. Embittered, blaming the Army for his situation, he had drifted westward. Of necessity, he had stolen food and, twice, horses. He had arrived in Kansas with the clothes on his back, an old fifty-caliber Maynard carbine and a Volcanic Arms .41 revolver—both taken from men he'd assaulted when they were drunk—and a horse with a suspiciously fresh brand mark.

For days, he had carefully watched the techniques of a bunco steerer and medicine show proprietor at a pitch stand in a small park near the state capitol in Topeka. Finally, Skaggs became confident that he knew all the moves and had memorized the patter. When the small-time confidence man packed up his wares and decamped in his swaying, high-centered wagon, at the insistence of the Topeka constabulary, Hiram Skaggs followed him westward.

On the third night of his journey to richer and safer fields of operation, Skaggs had joined the huckster at his campfire. After sharing the spurious "doctor's" bread, meat, and salt, Skaggs had risen up and murdered his host. A week later, having perfected the manual and vocal dexterity required to practice the shell game and the peddling of patent medicine, a new "Doctor Lyman Sanders" arrived in Junction City.

Big business could be done among the soldiers of nearby Fort Reilly. Only a few of the more astute and persistent idlers in the park near the center of town noticed that "Old Doc" had an unusually vehement hatred of the Army and nothing but contempt for the soldiers who comprised the bulk of his customers. Time and the law being immutables in the medicine show game, Skaggs eventually moved on to greener pastures.

For the next five years, the disgraced Union

officer plied his trade through Kansas and Nebraska. His wealth and girth grew rapidly. The stripes on his back, which had long ago become nothing more than a painful memory, caused him discomfort only when the weather became damp and cold. His detestation of the Army had not abated in the least. It had, in fact, become even more pronounced. By the time he had amassed a considerable stake in gold coin from sleight of hand and the sale of his remedy, and had swindled two elderly widows out of better than thirty thousand dollars, Hiram Skaggs decided the time had come to change professions.

Thus the Farmers' and Stockmen's Trust Bank of Dodge City had opened. He was respectable now, but his animosity toward the Army and all who filled its ranks never decreased. Located as he was, so near to Fort Dodge, constant contact with Army men only exacerbated the situation. When the raids had begun, he had envisioned a grand plan. How much better life would be when he had managed to carry it off. After pulling off the magnificent *coup* of this land transaction, he would embezzle the remaining funds in the bank and abscond to California to live out his life in luxury under a warm and hospitable sun. The droning report, he suddenly realized, had nearly come to an end.

"What do you mean she left with the Army?" he demanded.

"She climbed up on the supply wagon like she owned the damned thing, Mister Skaggs, and rode out toward Fort Dodge. O'Kelly was with her till the teamster rolled away. A bit after that, he an' that mule patrol rode off to the south."

"Damn, damn, damn," Skaggs mouthed nastily while he pounded his desk with a pudgy fist. "There's no way of—" He broke off, conscious of the ever-receptive ears of the indolent local who was his source of information.

"Get out of here," the banker snapped.

"What about my . . . uh, you know . . . ?"

Skaggs delved into a vest pocket and spun a three-dollar gold piece across the rosewood expanse of his desk. "Take it and go. See if you can find me some *good* news for a change."

Alone, his thoughts ranged back over the end of the informer's tale. Now that Susan was in the clutches of the accursed army, he could not further his designs on her, he thought furiously—nor could he immediately get revenge on that freckle-spotted bogtrotter, O'Kelly. But the time was coming. They'd see. They would all see.

Eli Holten had his bearings now. By his estimation, Fort Dodge lay only some ten miles away, give or take one or two. He felt certain that they had successfully managed to escape without detection. Alicia rode beside him, silent and determined. After a final check behind, the scout reined in.

"We need to rest the horses," he advised the girl.

"And . . . then we can—"

"No. We walk them while they cool out, then ride again."

Alicia rubbed at her own itching crotch. "I sorta hoped . . . Well, I ache all over for you, Eli. Can't we take a *little while?*"

"Errrumm," Holten returned neutrally. "Not just yet, Alicia. See that rock outcrop ahead. When we reach it, we can get back in the saddle."

"I got a saddle that sure wants to be gotten into," she returned sweetly.

A sudden chill coursed through the scout as he recalled another sweet-faced youngster who could never get enough of what she wanted most. Not even a band of raping Kiowa Apaches in the Texas Panhandle could slake her insatiable thirst for sexual delights. Despite his powerful will, even the scout had succumbed to her charms. Granted, Louise Van Pelton had come by her proclivities naturally—and nature had gone its course. That was not the case with the unfortunate Alicia. Victimized as a mere child, she had no standards by which to judge her behavior, and Holten feared her mind might be permanently damaged. This presented a far different situation—one the scout sincerely wished to be relieved of at the earliest possible opportunity. Consequently, in such meditative silence, he proceeded to walk beside the obviously aroused girl until they reached the jumble of weather-ravaged rocks.

"Let's mount up," Holten advised.

He and Alicia had barely set their feet in the stirrups when a pack of howling, teenage half-breed warriors erupted over the lip of a jagged-rimmed gulley. Firing their weapons indiscriminately, they rushed toward the trapped pair.

Holten bolted off Sonny's back and spun toward the menacing youths, a long finger of fire erupting from his Remington. Three fast shots put two of the attacking renegades on the ground, writhing in their death throes. Slowly, at the scout's direction, he and the girl pulled back into the shelter of the eroded boulders. Bullets sang deadly songs as they ricocheted off the rock, sending up showers of shards.

"Can you use this rifle?" Eli asked as he retrieved his Winchester from the saddle scabbard.

"Uh . . . yes."

A moment later when three of the charging hostiles swarmed up onto rocks, Alicia proved to be a deadly accurate shot. Holten accounted for one, while Alicia downed the others with rapid barks from the smoking rifle.

Her first victim took a .44-40 slug in the gut. He grunted, swayed and fell, both hands clutching his belly. Still spread atop the boulder, he tried to crawl to safety until he vomited up a large spew of blackish blood and shivered his way into death. Before he died, though, Alicia had plunked a second bullet into the hollow of another half-breed's throat.

The youngster managed only a short howl of pain; then he bent backward and toppled out of sight. Movement to the left behind the girl caused Eli to spin on one boot heel and send a sizzling round over her shoulder.

It struck flesh and brought a yowl of agony, though the young renegade held his place and tried to steady his rifle sights on Alicia's head.

Holten fired again. Blood and brain matter sprayed the air as the attacking mixed-blood took a .44 round from Holten's pistol in the right temple.

Even though the girl had proved to be an excellent shot, Holten realized the renegades had the upper hand. Time might not be on the attackers' side, with the fort so close, but their sheer numbers had to count for something.

Chapter Twelve

From atop the combination post office and city jail, the noontime bell clanged loudly through Cimarron. It sent many of the men home to their meals and the idlers out onto the street until establishments reopened following the usual hour of closure. Some farmers who had time on their hands became witnesses to the opening move in the complex and decidedly advanced plan of attack dreamed up by Charlie Roundtree, although at the time, they had no way of knowing that because the half-breeds rode into town singly or in small groups. Those who survived lived to regret this oversight.

But now these "spit an' whittlers" watched warily, while a total of a dozen men entered their town. The strangers spread out, heading in different directions. Three, however, stopped at the livery, where one engaged the blacksmith next door in conversation over the cost of shoeing his horse.

The last to enter was Joe Sureshot. He rode the length of the main street, then turned and started back. This was the signal for the others to act.

Six-guns barked at the livery and the hostler and blacksmith fell dead. Quickly two renegades ran inside and set fire to the stored hay. A trio of hardcase quarter-bloods kicked in the door to the general mercantile. They, too, preceded their entrance with a fusillade of hot lead.

Attracted by the gunfire, the town marshal rushed into the street, a snowy napkin still tucked in the front of his shirt. This was what Joe had been waiting for. He kicked his mount to a gallop and bore down on the lawman. As the marshal started to draw his weapon, two other breeds gunned him down from behind.

Blood spurted from the front of the marshal's chest, staining his shirt and the napkin crimson as bits of bone and lung tissue flew through the air. Ripped by five shots, the lawman staggered forward and then crumpled in a heap. A large puff of dust rose around his inert form. Beyond him, glass tinkled musically as one renegade jumped his horse through the big front window of the only saloon in town.

Shouts came from inside, along with the bark of the half-breed's revolver. A shotgun boomed and two more six-guns crackled to life. At once, more of the marauders charged the violated façade of the establishment, quickly ending the resistance within.

This is the fun part, Joe Sureshot thought to himself. Like the old days of raiding with his mother's family in the Osage band. He looked beyond the chaos to a point outside of town.

There, Charlie Roundtree had perfectly aligned the remainder of his powerful force in a classic cavalry formation, horns pointed forward at the ends, its center backed into a concave shape that would allow any enemy to be surrounded and closed in upon with no chance of escape. Across the distance, he heard Charlie's steady voice speak the chilling command.

"Bugler, sound the charge!"

A glissando of brassy notes cascaded from the bell of the valveless instrument and the whole of that fearsome wave started forward. With the center of town as their target, the yelling horsemen raced across the ground drifting wildly at any fleeing figures they chanced to observe, a thick cloud of dust rising in their wake.

Accustomed as he had become to watching it, in drill and in practice, the awesome sight sent shivers up Joe's spine. This time their target was a whole town, not an isolated farm. The snap and buzz of bullets passing close by his head brought Joe back to his surroundings.

A number of locals had rallied and started to return fire. No longer a one-sided affair, the battle quickly became heated. Rifles crackled from windows, their users concealed behind curtains and heavy drapes. A shotgun boomed heavily from the doorway of a butcher shop. With deadly precision, a spray of bullets came from the small square opening atop the grain elevator.

Three of the attackers took hits from an unseen sharpshooter far above and fell screaming from their mounts.

By that time the full brunt of the charging riders had struck the town. Women screamed and ran to gather up their stray children. Too late for one ponderously fat mother.

As she swayed, shook and waddled after a fleeing five-year-old, two of the hooting warriors thundered down on her. Bending low to each of her corpulent sides, they hooked forearms under her armpits and yanked her from the ground.

At a full gallop, they pounded toward a distant tie rail at the corner where the main street and the narrow side lane in which they had plucked her off her feet intersected. Once lined up properly, they held their course until the last second, then veered slightly as they released their blubbery burden.

Shrieking in terror, the woman flew through the air and collided with the deep-set upright at one end of the hitchrail. Her head made a chopped-melon *plock* as it struck, showering the street and building front with a watery mush of blood, fluid, and pulped brain tissue. Mindlessly, her legs continued to churn and her pointed-toe, ankle-high shoes drummed the ground.

Now, the assault fanned throughout the town as black smoke, tinged with white, began to rise from the grain elevator. Still, the determined sniper remained in place and rapidly eliminated five more half-breed predators.

Joe Sureshot found Charlie Roundtree at his side. "Watch this," the leader declared, an index finger pointed at the elevator. "Any time now."

Suddenly the metal walls of the structure bulged outward. A series of muffled *wha-whumps* sounded from within. Then a cataclysmic blast disintegrated the grain elevator into fragmented shards of flying metal, wood, and grain.

Though light in weight and, consequently, short in range, the wheat scythed through three defenders crouched near the blast like so much quail shot. Their blood leaked from hundreds of tiny wounds and the cumulative pain level, like that from a shotgun blast, short-circuited their nervous systems and they died of massive shock.

Whistling through the air, long slivers of wood and jagged-edged chunks of tin siding democratically cut down friend and foe alike. An instant after the explosion, which had unhorsed fully a third of the raiders with its blast and enormous ground shock, a dozen new bodies littered the main street of Cimarron.

"Wasn't that beautiful!" Charlie Roundtree screamed, himself, like many others, temporarily deafened by the tremendous explosion. *"Beautiful!"*

"With that . . . blast . . ." Joe gasped out, robbed of his breath by the spectacular upheaval, "an' by the time we kill ever'one, the white settlers oughtta be a-scramblin' all the way back to the Mississippi River."

· "We don't have to kill them all," Charlie

assured him. "Only steal everything we can haul away and burn down the rest. Any survivors will spread stories of what we've done to this place and that will panic people like fear of the plague."

Joe turned away, toward the church, from which came the shrieks and wails of frightened women and children. "Round up them women!" he yelled to some idling raiders. "Round 'em up and let's get some fucking started!"

Random shooting and killing went on for most of the day. The remaining raiders still outnumbered the townsfolk by an easy three to one. The men and older youths who resisted the ravaging of their community were hunted out singly or in small groups and blasted into broken, bleeding flesh that littered the ground like carrion in a slaughter house. Finally opposition became suicidal.

Sobbing men and boys watched helplessly from their covers as the savage mixed-bloods raped their wives and daughters, mothers and sisters. Several, unable to endure this humiliating torment, broke from their hiding places and rushed the two-legged beasts sating themselves in the streets on the tender flesh of their loved ones. With raging growls deep in their throats they threw themselves on the despoilers, only to die of knife slashes and point-blank gunshots.

Aloof from the mundane squalor of violated white flesh, Charlie Roundtree supervised the loading of whiskey, food, and general goods from the mercantile and saloon. Fine saddles, sets of harness, and all manner of livery accessories came from the leathersmith's shop and the surviving outbuildings at the stables. Rifles, shotguns, six-guns, and case-lots of ammunition came from a small gunsmithy and tin shop. Huge smiles decorated the faces of the men conducting the systematic looting. Like their leader, they knew of the enormous profits these items could bring, once the renegade scare had ended and gullible whites once more poured into this semiarid land. For Charlie, it meant even more.

Land for sale by the square section. Miles and miles of it. Thousands . . . no, millions of dollars in his pocket. Given time, he knew these worthless dregs of two cultures would begin to quarrel among themselves, fights would break out, and men would die. The band would split up, each going his own way. And Charlie Roundtree would be left behind to reap the rewards of diligent planning and careful execution. How he reveled in this knowledge.

By an hour before sundown, the last rapable woman had been dug out of hiding and violated until she bled profusely from her savaged nether parts. A few of the children had been ripped asunder by the bulging organs of those who had a taste for young stuff and no concern for what that did to their victims. Then Charlie Roundtree inspected the town, well satisfied. The wagons were already on the way back to his camp. Five bottles of whiskey per man had been distributed to the surviving raiders. The time to leave had come.

"Light torches!" Charlie commanded. "Let's

burn this place to the ground. Everyone mount up. Bugler, sound 'Boots and Saddles'!"

"They'll be coming back," Eli Holten told Alicia while they watched the last fine spurts of dust disburse from the sandy slope in front of them.

"We're about out of bullets."

"Cartridges," the scout automatically corrected her. "There's ammunition right out there. I'm going to get some of it. Take a good long drink. Then get some of that jerked buffalo and the wild onions you brought along. We should eat something while we have the chance."

At Holten's urging, Alicia complied. She seemed sane enough, the scout mused as he moved among the rocks toward the corpses of their attackers. Except for her obsession with sex. He paused near one roughly egg-shaped boulder and relieved a dead half-breed of a beltlike bandoleer of .44-40 rounds. Only a boy, he thought with regret as he moved on.

A few feet away, another body lay sprawled in death. From the loops of a pistol belt, Eli took nine rounds, three more from the cylinder of the Merwin and Hulbert that lay in the dirt a few inches from an open, relaxed palm. This one, he observed, had been hardly more than a child.

"Raise up your children in the ways of their fathers." This, the scout reflected sourly as he looked at the lives snuffed out far too early, was not

what the Bible had in mind. He came to a third corpse and bent low.

"Eli, look out!" The shout came from their stronghold.

Instantly, he heard the crack of a bullet—fired from the Winchester in Alicia's hands—and a meaty smack behind him as hot lead plowed into human flesh.

Only a weak whimper came from the youthful renegade who crumpled among the rocks, blood bubbling from his tightly clenched lips. Quickly the scout gathered up the twenty rounds at hand and hurried back to the girl.

"They've changed tactics," he informed her. "They'll try to sneak up on us from our blind side. Be ready." He reached for a piece of buffalo jerky that was soaking to softness in a small cast-iron pot, and began to munch on it.

"The onions are sweet," Alicia observed.

"Best time of the year for them," Eli told her as he crunched one of the aromatic bulbs between strong, white teeth. "Later there will be wild turnips and hot peppers."

"I hope we live to taste them," the girl remarked with a shudder.

Brown bodies sprang into view amidst the rocks that had been at their backs. One of the young mixed-bloods snapped off a shot that screeched demonically when it knocked over the cooking vessel and ricocheted away, smashed out of shape by the convex outer surface of the iron pot. Eli triggered his Remington.

Two-hundred-five grains of lead, propelled at

about seven hundred feet per second, shoved the boy backward and doubled him over. Beside Eli, the Winchester cracked angrily. Suddenly the teenaged renengades came at them from every point.

Howling and screaming, the diminutive warriors closed in. Holten emptied his revolver and drew his Bowie as Alicia fired mechanically, cool and steady. Three more of the attacking force fell before their leader unwisely withdrew.

"Reload," Holten snapped. "Quickly. They'll be back."

His prediction proved true.

In a matter of minutes, the determined half-breed youths charged once more. Lead screamed and howled off the rocks. Alicia rose to take advantage of the waning light and get a better field of fire.

Four slugs ripped into her body, jerking and twisting her so that she performed a grim dance of death before she slammed into a boulder and slid to a sitting position. Blood ran from her mouth and ears, and seeped from ghastly exit wounds on the front and back of her chest and abdomen.

"Damn! Oh, damn it all," the scout cursed furiously. He continued to fire, once more running his Remington dry. With a swift sideways dodge, he snatched up the Winchester and continued the battle.

Two struggling boys wedged themselves between a pair of boulders as they strove to reach the hated scout. Eli punched one round apiece into them. So tightly packed had they become, they did not fall, even in death. He worked the lever of the Winchester and whirled at a rattling sound close behind him.

The hammer fell and a loud click followed as the firing pin snapped forward on an empty chamber. A tall, brawny lad of perhaps sixteen faced the scout, a wild grin on his face, his lips drawn back in a rictus of blood lust. Almost contemptuously he raised the barrel of an old model percussion Colt.

Before he could squeeze the trigger, the scout reacted with blinding speed. Turning the rifle sideways in his grip, he struck forward with the steel-capped butt. The shock of the impact jarred Eli's wrists and forearms, but he felt a satisfying gritty give as teeth and jawbone splintered under his lateral butt stroke.

"Take him alive! Take him alive!" a voice shouted from Holten's left.

Another tactical error, the scout thought to himself. Youth and inexperience made for a poor commander of any sort of troops. He moved in on another of the renegades, feinted with the butt of the Winchester, then swung, driving the muzzle deep into the hollow of the boy's throat.

Muscle tore and cartilage crackled. The young half-breed made a strangled sound and fell backward, his face pale, blood already seeping from his lips. Then the survivors overwhelmed Holten.

Eli spun in a tight circle, swinging the rifle like a club to keep some distance between him and his nearly victorious captors. Two burly teenagers

160

were preparing to leap him from behind when whirring, whiplike cracks signaled that bullets had split the air close by the scout's body.

Ugly red blossoms appeared on the youthful pair's chests and they fell away. In the same instant, Holten hit the ground and a fusillade erupted over him. As the remaining half-breeds broke off their attack and ran for their lives, a familiar, tall figure rose from the tossing swale of buffalo grass some thirty yards away. He came rolling toward the scout in the familiar stride of a cavalryman.

"Sure an' what 'tis it yer doin' out here, playin' games with these children, Mister Holten?"

"O'Kelly!" Eli cried as he came to his feet. "I sure could have used you half an hour ago."

The Irish noncom chuckled low in his throat as he stepped closer. "An' if it would please yez, we could go back and let 'em have another try at yez."

"Never mind."

O'Kelly sniffed curiously and wrinkled his nose. "What the devil is that hideous stench?"

"Wild onions."

"Were ye tryin' to kill them blood-thirsty brats off with yer breath?"

"It got that close," the scout allowed through a relieved smile.

"Ye haven't answered me first question as yet."

"No time. I'll explain everything when we reach Lieutenant Stone. We have to ride like a wind out of hell."

"Why's that?"

"I've been a captive of the renegades. They set

161

out early this morning to raid a couple of towns. Cimarron and Haggard to be specific."

"That's a lot o' miles to cover from here," O'Kelly observed.

"We'll have to do it, even if we run those mules into the ground. A lot of people are going to die if we don't."

Chapter Thirteen

A thick pall of smoke still hung over Cimarron a little before noon the next day when Eli Holten and Lieutenant Stone led the patrol into the town. The heavy air, thick with the stench of blood, death, and destruction, vibrated with the wails of the grieving and the wounded. Unaccountably, a few of the village mongrels had survived to growl and yap an unfriendly greeting at the soldiers as they walked their mounts through the heaps of ashes that had been homes, businesses, and a house of worship.

"My God, did they use dynamite?" Lieutenant Stone inquired when he came in sight of the shallow pit that had once been the grain elevator.

"Nope," Eli speculated. He next quoted an Army ordnance officer whom he had heard lecturing on explosives. "Grain dust, mixed with the right portion of air, is highly explosive. It has a power three times that of the same weight of dynamite."

"These poor people," the young officer remarked quietly as he waved an arm to encompass the staggering, zombielike inhabitants of Cimarron, now threading their way through the desolation.

Here and there one would pause to lift a charred or soot-covered corpse from the ruins. Only gradually did their numbed brains realize that the Army had arrived. Without consultation, they left off their grisly, doleful activities and converged on the shock-hushed troops. None spoke until they had ringed the soldiers around.

"Why weren't you here to protect us?" The question came out as an angry snarl from the former owner of the saddle shop.

"Yeah, why?" a woman demanded in a quavering voice. "My . . . my babies are all dead because the Army wasn't here."

"Our homes are destroyed, our businesses wiped out. Those renegade bastards looted the place of everything that wasn't bolted down," the mayor of Cimarron said accusingly while he clutched a wounded shoulder.

Angry mutters rose into a chorus and the people moved in closer, as if to take their revenge on these saviors who had failed them. Eli Holten rose in his stirrups.

"Folks! Listen to me." Shouts of rage and misery drowned him out. Eli drew his Remington and fired a shot into the air.

"I said to listen. There's no time for whining and bickering. There'll be time enough later to fix blame. The soldiers here only knew you were in danger by nightfall yesterday. They've come a long way and we have a lot farther to go."

"Why?" a surly man who had been the manager of the grain elevator demanded.

"I know for a fact that the renegades are headed for Haggard right now. We might be able to outrun them. They will be slowed by the wagons they took from here. If we do, we can help Haggard defend itself from their attack."

"A lot of good that does us."

"Right!"

"Who cares about Haggard? Look what they done to our town."

"And you'd stand by and let them do it to another place?" the scout countered scornfully. "Why, I've seen more loyalty and brotherly feeling among the Sioux and Cheyenne than any of you possess. These half-breeds burned your town, killed your friends and family, and had their way with your women, unless I miss my guess; yet you only want to stand around and snivel about it and blame the Army. Don't you want revenge?

"If any of you who are able will arm yourselves and ride with us, we might be able to save Haggard from the same fate, or at least catch the renegades between our guns and those of that town, and wipe them out to the last man."

A couple of men shouted approval, but the mayor, with trembling lips, voiced the opinion of the majority, or at least what he thought that to be.

"W-we ain't got no choice but to tend to our wounds, pack what we can, and leave this terrible place, mister."

"That's right," another defeated townie joined in. "We got better things to do than go chasin' off after an army of renegades that even you soldiers don't seem too anxious to get close to."

"What!" Eli thundered. "Where's your balls? Uh, pardon me ladies. Did the breeds take them too?"

"You callin' us yellah?"

"Yes, I am," the scout growled. "The way you talk, you haven't got a set of nuts among you. What did you do when they came in here? 'Oh, please come in and take all you want.' 'Try my wife . . . *pretty please.*'"

"Why you son of a bitch!" A suddenly angry townie made a try for the six-gun tucked in his waistband, only to find himself looking down the unwavering muzzle of Holten's Remington. The hammer lay back and ready.

"Easy, Eli," Lieutenant Stone advised cautiously, while he, too, rested his hand on the butt of his service revolver.

"Ah-hem," a merchant who still wore the tatters of a silk vest cleared his throat and then spoke lightly. "They won't be in too big a hurry. They cleaned out my saloon of all its liquor. The one in charge passed out five bottles apiece to his men. Some of them were already downing it as they rode out."

"You see. We do have a chance," Eli appealed to

the crowd once again.

"Count me in," the tough-looking elevator manager declared.

"Me, too," another man volunteered.

Amid the commotion, the reverend of the local church rushed up. His pale face bore a perplexed expression and his hands trembled as he rubbed them together. "I . . . I've been through most of the ashes of the church. Th-there ain't any bones. They didn't burn our women alive . . . they took 'em."

Bellows of anger rose from the gathering.

"We'll go! We'll all go," the saloon keeper exclaimed.

Ever sober, Charlie Roundtree watched with disgusted frustration as his men abandoned any pretense of discipline and gave themselves over to the revels of their victory. Only fifteen miles from Cimarron, yet they had spent the whole of the night in drinking and abusing the captive women. They should be riding against Haggard right now, swarming into the streets to wipe the stupid, helpless white men from the earth.

"We have to move!" Charlie shouted aloud. "The Army will hear about Cimarron and come after us. We have a plan to follow," he reminded his throbbing-headed followers. They only gazed back in red-eyed agony, hangovers pounding at their temples.

At his side, Joe Sureshot chuckled and blinked equally bleary eyes. "Don't worry, Charlie. Without the scout to help, any chance of the Army being able to track us isn't worth spit. Those blue-bellies couldn't find their butts with a bull fiddle."

"No, damn it. This is not the way. We've only forty-seven men left and they're all drunk. We're falling apart, Joe." He strode off angrily and kicked at the bare buttocks of a drunken breed who humped lazily at the unprotesting body of a woman from Cimarron.

Snarling angrily, the mixed-blood withdrew his reddened penis and curled up into a ball. Then, within seconds, he began to snore.

"Get up! Damn you! All of you, on your feet!" the leader roared. "Bugler, sound 'Assembly'."

"Guh! Unnnh," the white renegade muttered and dropped back into besotted slumber.

"Joe, help me. Gather up the women and we'll put them in the wagon. I'll take them back to the camp. While I'm gone, get these useless sacks of shit on their feet and on the way to Haggard. We'll attack there in the morning."

"If you say so, Charlie. But I would sure like another go at that li'l yellow-haired one before you do."

"Oooh!" Charlie moaned in utter disgust.

"Cimarron's been wiped out!" the wild-eyed man yelled as he galloped the length of Dodge City's main street. "Renegades burned the place to the ground."

"What's this?" Ed Masterson demanded as he stepped through the batwings of the Oasis Saloon.

168

"It's a fact, Marshal. Those raiders is hittin' towns now. God knows, Dodge might be next. There's a reg'lar army of 'em."

"Calm down and tell me the details."

"It's awful. Kilt most of the men, blew up the grain elevator. I heard they took the women off with them."

Word spread rapidly. Milling crowds began to form, the largest in front of the Farmers' and Stockmen's Trust Bank. Inside, a beaming Hiram Skaggs sat behind his desk, on which he was rapidly piling papers as he passed out stacks of gold and silver coin in exchange for the deeds and titles to one farm after another.

By nightfall, he had also obtained titles to many houses and smaller businesses in Dodge City. Still the line did not shorten.

"Hiram, I'd like a word with you," Anton Mueller, principal trustee of the bank demanded.

"Not now, Anton. Too busy. We're doin' a land-office business here." Skaggs laughed in a high, braying cackle at his own poor joke.

"That's what has us worried. Are you doing any bank business?"

"Of course. The tellers are handling that."

"Mostly withdrawals, I note," another trustee observed in a sour tone.

"First thing in the morning, we're going to check the books, Hiram," Mueller announced. "You had better not be buying property with anyone's money but your own. We don't condone this rush to sell out. Not good for the community, or the bank. You had better see everything is

169

in order."

"Oh, it will be, it will be," Skaggs told them cheerily.

He had little reason to fear an audit, he reminded himself as he grinned down at the solemn faces of the trustees. He had hidden his chiseling deep in the lined pages of the ledgers. It would take weeks . . . months, to discover how he'd managed to shift all those funds to his own account. By then he would be on top, with money to burn. His plan was moving smoothly toward completion. The panic had spread even better than he had predicted.

Soon now, he would be in a position to make millions. The Army could not stand by now. The renegades would be driven off and the people would come back. He had dropped the price to five cents on the dollar. Oh, God, how much money I will make, he gloated. Long before an audit could be completed, the selling would start again. He'd easily have tens of thousands with which to make payoffs to the trustees. Let them get a sniff of some solid, untraceable gold coin and they'd stop their whining about ethics.

Why at a dime an acre over the proper market value of all that land, the trustees could get rich, too, off the very people he was busily skinning right now. Oh, yes, Hiram chortled gleefully to himself. What a blessing this renegade uprising had been.

Chapter Fourteen

"Civilian volunteers are formed up and ready, sir," Sergeant O'Kelly told Lieutenant Stone, his hand rigidly against the visor of his kepi in a snappy salute.

"Very good, Sergeant. Mister Holten, you will scout for the civilians and lead them in the attack," the young officer told Eli with grave formality.

"Yes, sir."

"I will take the troops along the road to Haggard. If you encounter the hostiles at any distance from their intended target, engage them and attempt to draw them off from the town."

"Yes, sir." Eli found it hard to suppress a grin. "If you don't mind, Lieutenant, I have an idea that might work out to our best advantage."

"What is that?"

The scout took Lieutenant Stone aside and quickly outlined his plan. It involved several tricky and dangerous aspects, which the officer accepted reluctantly. Included in the overview was a unique way to defend Haggard, provided they got there in time. When Eli had concluded, Stone grinned appreciatively and gave his hearty approval.

"We'll do that, then. Good luck, Eli."

"Same to you, Rick. We'll need all we can get."

Long into the night, Eli and the men of Cimarron trailed the renegades crosscountry, while the moon gave off an eerie silver light that frosted the undulating, sandy ground and made shadows into pools of ink. The scout sensed that they had covered many miles. They had found the previous night's campsite of the renegades and had studied the scuffed ground for some indication of what to expect from Charlie Roundtree's marauders.

"That wagon was sure heavy loaded," one citizen of Cimarron remarked as he examined the ruts beside Holten.

"Probably with your women."

"Then we ought to be headin' in that direction."

"No. We have a job to do first. There's nothing but women and kids in that camp. No more harm will befall the women if we crush these half-breeds before they can get back there."

Eli met less resistance from the townsmen than he'd expected, so under the light of the full moon, he and his small command rode on toward

172

Haggard, pulled forward by the tantalizing sign of the horses that had preceded them. After explaining the meaning of the trail sign that was guiding them to a quick-witted town dweller, Holten rode ahead to scout the ground between the column and their enemy.

A half hour's ride brought the scout within about five miles of Haggard. As he scanned the horizon in every direction, the dull glow of several fires hidden in a deep ravine caught his attention. A mile or better to the south of his present course, he knew it must be the hostile camp. Holten walked Sonny to within a quarter mile of it and then dismounted.

He exchanged his boots for soft, silent-walking Sioux moccasins. As a precaution, he slid his Winchester from the scabbard and started off, a pair of Army-issue field glasses swung around his neck. His casual, circuitous approach finally brought him to a point where he could study the gully while remaining unobserved. Carefully he eased himself into position and lifted the field glasses.

Moving figures sprang into focus as he twisted the knob. For the most part he saw dark men, with long black hair, hawk noses, and squat bodies, their legs bowed from a lifetime of horseback riding. Here and there, he also spotted others with dusky skins and yellow locks. He had found the half-breeds.

The cocky renegades seemed to fear nothing as they heaped brush onto their huge fires and talked or gambled noisily amongst themselves. All of the marauders swilled endlessly from whiskey bottles —many empty ones had been found along their trail—but careful scrutiny revealed that his supposition had been correct. He saw no sign of the captive white women. However, he noted with surprise the presence of sentries on horseback. They guarded the perimeter of the camp, and four of them patrolled the rim of the ravine. Indians rarely had guards.

Despite the laxity inside the camp, the scout noted the military precision in its layout, also in the activities of the lookouts. He gave grudging, silent respect to Charlie Roundtree's ability to whip this motley crew into line. Patiently he began to count.

Forty-seven men. Far too many of the savage mixed-bloods for his small contingent to take on, even in a night raid. Besides, the women—their true objective—were not there. It was obvious that the raiders were in no hurry, so satisfied with his evaluation of the situation, Holten made ready to withdraw. First, however, he quickly formulated another plan.

To his way of seeing things, the men of Cimarron might be able to have their cake and eat it. Cautiously he eased himself back from the edge and beyond the point where he could be spotted by the drinking, carousing breeds below. Once out of their view, he rose and turned to head for where he'd left Sonny ground-reined to graze—only to run into the barrel-like chest of a horse.

"Hunnnh!" the half-breed atop the beast grunted. A thud and soft gurgle followed the surprised sentry's exclamation. Soaked to the gills, the scout had thought in a flash and he'd reacted swiftly, swinging the barrel of his Winchester.

The hard steel tube had connected with the side of the guard's head and the half-breed had fallen from his saddle into the tall grass, his temple bone splintered. His pony excitedly danced a few steps away, then began to graze. Holten hurried through the night to his own mount.

Twenty minutes later he rejoined the column of volunteers.

"I've found them. It looks like they're settled in for the night. I think we have time to accomplish something else before we have to close in for the kill. Jamie," he called to a young boy who had accompanied the column in search of his sister.

When the youngster came to his side, Eli explained what he wanted. "Jamie, ride toward Haggard. Find Lieutenant Stone and tell him that the renegades are camped five miles from town, to the southeast. There're forty-seven of them. They are still drinking and whooping it up. Charlie Roundtree is not with them. He must be on the wagon with the women. Tell the lieutenant we are going after the wagon and will try to intercept it, free the women and be in position before dawn to attack the enemy's rear. You've got all of that?"

"Yeah," the wide-eyed lad said in an awed tone. "We're gonna get the womenfolk back, then kick butt on those red niggers."

"Something like that," Eli agreed dryly. "Only be sure you tell the lieutenant exactly what I told you. Word for word."

Jamie repeated the message to Eli, who nodded in satisfaction.

"All right, men," the scout told the other residents of Cimarron, "we are starting out after that wagon as soon as Jamie here gets on his way."

A ragged, if quiet, cheer rose from the vengeful husbands and fathers.

Men poured through the dimly lighted streets of Haggard like ants around their hill at the start of a rainstorm. Wagons stood before almost every business establishment and home on the three residential avenues. Women chattered shrilly as they labored to pack dusty trunks recently recovered from storage places. Babies cried, unattended, while their mothers worked frantically to bundle bedding and fine china into the backs of waiting buggies. Older children, confused by the frantic activity, ran about shouting in shrill voices, chasing each other through the teeming clots of frightened adults.

Word of what had happened in Cimarron had reached the small farming community. No one wanted to wait around for a similar fate. The sounds of pounding hoofbeats, approaching out of the dark, galvanized the disorganized herd of harried people into purposeful action.

Guns bristled from windows and behind buckboards. Silence, except for the occasional fretful wail of an infant, settled over the town. If a keen-eyed citizen had not called out in time, a tragedy would have occurred.

"Hey! It's the Army. The soldiers has got here!" the vigilant Haggardite shouted as Lieutenant Stone and his men cantered into town.

People came from everywhere and swarmed around the mule corps as it slackened to a walk and proceeded to the center of town. There Stone reined in and looked about him. Young Jamie Peters sat his shaggy pony at the officer's side.

This will never do, Stone thought to himself. These people have begun to pack for flight. He looked over at Sergeant O'Kelly.

"Sure an' we got about two seconds to stop a stampede, Lieutenant."

"Right you are, Sergeant. What do you suggest?"

"Well, now, I recommend we proceed under Article Ninety-nine, sir."

"There isn't any Article Ninety-nine, O'Kelly. There're only ninety-eight Articles of War."

O'Kelly gave him a long, conspiratorial wink. "Sure an' the Lieutenant's forgettin', sir. *Article Ninety-nine*, the one about temporary martial law."

"Oh! Oh, yes. Now I remember. That sounds like just the thing to do."

Richard Stone dismounted and strode, in what he hoped would appear a purposeful manner, to a nearby buckboard that stood under a street lantern. As he climbed onto the wagon box, a woman's nearly hysterical voice bleated from across the street.

"Oh, they've come to lead us to safety. Praise the Lord!"

Two dozen voices, all tinged with panic, were raised in a babble of confused shouts and cries for assistance. Lieutenant Stone let them go on for a moment, then he took a deep breath to brace himself. He drew his Smith and Wesson Schofield service revolver and fired a round moonward.

Silence struck like the dawn of Judgment Day.

"You people aren't going anywhere!"

Another torrent of protest rose in frightened waves from the gathering knot of residents. From behind them, where he sat with the troops, Sergeant O'Kelly triggered off a .44 slug that clanged ominously off the bell in the church steeple.

"Jesus, Mary an' Joseph, an' all the saints. Forgive me my sin," O'Kelly muttered as he crossed himself.

His act of accidental sacrilege brought quiet, though.

"What do you mean, Lieutenant?" a strained voice finally asked.

"What I said. You people are not going anywhere. The renegades are five miles southeast of here. They are going to hit Haggard in the morning."

"Then what are you wastin' time for yammerin' at us about not going anywhere?" a frightened man blurted out. "Let's get goin'."

"This is the third time. I won't say it again." The big Schofield in his hand emphasized his intent in the event someone debated the point. "No one goes anywhere. The renegades are going to attack. That is a fact. This is too." Again Richard Stone drew a deep breath to bolster his courage because what he was about to say and what he and his men would be doing in the next few hours were as illegal as anything could be.

"Under the authority of Article Ninety-nine of the Articles of War, I declare Haggard to be under temporary martial law. Every able-bodied man and boy over fifteen will report back here within ten minutes with weapon and ammunition in hand. Then we will prepare the defenses of the town."

"We're peace-loving folk hereabouts," a pudgy young man, made soft by easy living and overprotection, complained. "We don't believe in all of this terrible violence."

"Ye'd better start then," Sergeant O'Kelly told the protestor nastily. "Else when them renegades gits here tomorra mornin', ye'll be dead . . . dead . . . dead."

"Any person attempting to leave the area under martial law without permission or found shirking his duty, will be shot," Stone hastened to add, to strengthen his point.

"You don't think these soldier boys will kill their own kind in cold blood, do you, Lieutenant?" a dandified individual sneered.

Slowly Richard Stone raised the Smith and Wesson .45 until the black hole in its muzzle was centered between the offensive youth's soft, brown eyes. "I, personally, will kill any man who fails to abide by the regulations. Do you want to be first?"

"You wouldn't dare . . ."

Though not a loud sound, the click of the Schofield seemed shattering as Stone thumbed back the hammer. The cylinder rotated and placed a soft gray slug in line with the barrel. Oily sweat suddenly broke out on the foppish young man's forehead. His eyes rolled up and he wilted to the ground in a swoon.

"Women and children to the three strongest buildings in town. Those who can handle firearms will be issued them. The others will prepare food, coffee, and bandages. Boys eight to fifteen will organize a bucket brigade to handle fires. Get moving; you have ten minutes."

As swiftly as they had gathered, the civilians vanished into the night.

"O'Kelly, position the men to make sure no one attempts to run out. If any do, shoot above them or at them, but don't shoot to kill."

"Aye, sir. We need every man Jack of 'em, we do." O'Kelly slapped his thigh. "By all the saints, Lieutenant, I think ye might carry this off."

"I can sincerely say that I devoutly hope so."

Although not the most comfortable of lodgings, the one-room cabin provided for Susan Walters by the colonel's lady proved to be adequate and secure. Susan settled in and dismissed Hiram Skaggs from her mind. Eli Holten wasn't so easy to put aside, however. Susan had to admit she was worried sick about him. A knock at the door brought her to her feet, heart pounding.

Silly girl, she chided herself. Yet she couldn't help but hope that beyond that solid pine portal stood the smiling, handsome scout. She hurried forward to open it.

An orderly stood outside, hat off, a stained and wrinkled envelope in one hand. "Letter, ma'am," he mumbled apologetically. "Sorry to disturb you so late."

"No trouble, Private. Thank you. How did it come so late?"

"Hand delivered to the main gate, ma'am."

"When? By whom?"

"Don't know, ma'am. I'm assigned to the provost office for tonight. The corporal of the guard brought it in and told me to fetch it on over here to you."

Susan took the envelope and noted her name had been inscribed on the outside in a firm, broad stroke. Quickly she tore it open and unfolded the single sheet of foolscap it contained.

"Oh!" Susan unconsciously exclaimed when she saw that the note had been signed by the scout. Swiftly her eyes scanned the few lines.

I am in need of your help. I am wounded and cannot come to the fort. I suspect that someone high up there is in cahoots with the renegades. Come as soon as you can.

Love
Eli

A chill washed through the lovely young woman, and for a moment her courage left her. Then she girded up her resolve with a deep breath and turned pleading eyes on the youthful soldier.

"Is there any way you can arrange transportation for me, Private? I'm in desperate need of a way back to Dodge City."

"At this time of night?" He started to protest, but seeing the stubborn determination in her firm jawline and blazing eyes, he swallowed. "A . . . ah . . . mule is about the only thing, ma'am. Awful uncomfortable for a lady, if you don't mind my sayin' so."

Susan gave him a winning smile. "It will do fine. And . . . Private . . . don't tell a soul about this."

"Oh, I can't do that, ma'am. The corporal of the guard will have to know in order to let you out the gate."

"All right, then. Him and no one else. But hurry. I must get going."

An hour had gone by in Haggard. During that time wagons had been jammed into the outward mouths of alleys; and barricades of rigs, buggies, and barrels of flour, beans, and pickles had sealed off the wider streets. In the midst of these hurried preparations, Sgt. Clerance O'Kelly approached a harried Lieutenant Stone.

"Sir, there's somethin' ye need to see out here."

"What's that, Sergeant. I'm busier than a supply

182

clerk on reissue day."

"If ye don't mind steppin' outside, sir, I've a few fellers I'm sure you want to meet."

Outside the stout brick bank building, which the lieutenant had commandeered for a command post, three infantrymen guarded five dark-skinned, surly men with long, ragged black hair. They wore mismatched assortments of clothing, but each had a relatively new pair of Army boots.

"Well, well. Who have we here, Sergeant?"

"Me boys caught these slitherin' snakes attemptin' to slip outta town. Rather than get their heads blowed off, they gave up all peaceable like. By the looks of 'em, they ain't townfolk, sir."

"Nooo," Stone drawled out. "No, I think they might work for Charlie Roundtree. What about it, men? You part of Charlie's renegade army?"

"Put lance in back-hole, blue-belly chief," the first snarled.

A rifle butt in his left kidney dropped the defiant captive to his knees.

"What about you?" Stone asked the man next in line.

"He was trying to tell you to go fuck yourself, Lieutenant."

Two solid blows from the butts of Springfields put that one down and out.

"Were you on the way to warn Charlie?" the youthful officer asked pointedly of the third renegade.

"You all die. Charlie Roundtree kill all whites, bring back buffalo."

183

Bright lights exploded in the fanatical half-breed's head when O'Kelly cuffed his ear with the barrel of a Schofield .45.

"You look like you're willing to tell us what we want to know," Stone told the fourth brigand.

Thick lips worked for a moment, then the mixed-blood spat a gobbet of slimy mucus full in the lieutenant's face.

A bright flash of light preceded the eruption of the back of the renegade's head. The report from O'Kelly's Smith and Wesson echoed off the clapboard buildings that framed the alley. Part of the nasty effluvium sprayed into the face of the remaining prisoner.

"You can't do that. That against law. You have much trouble."

"You were on your way to Charlie Roundtree, right? What time does he intend to attack this town?"

"No talk. Fuck you, soldier."

At a nod from O'Kelly, three Springfield butts began to thud and smash into the renegade. He fell, only to be pounded more. After a while, when he quit moving, the beating ended, along with his life.

"That's a little excessive, isn't it, Sergeant?" Lieutenant Stone asked offhandedly.

"One of these bastards is a Tonk, remember, Lieutenant. A damned, black-hearted cannibal. You saw what they've done. Do you really think their brand of terror needs to be treated according to the Articles of War?"

"Control your emotions, Sergeant. But . . . confidentially, no. I can't think of anything too bad to do to them."

"And, at least, sir, the enemy won't get any o' the latest news."

"There is that. . . ."

Chapter Fifteen

Piercing rays from the bloated red-orange ball on the eastern horizon assaulted Joe Sureshot's head and split it like a pea. The great accumulation of woolly numbness inside his skull shifted lethargically as Joe sat upright. He rubbed gritty eyes and licked a parched tongue over cracked, sandpaper lips. His stomach roiled with acid fire and the world spun in dizzying spirals as he tried to maintain his equilibrium. Involuntarily his hands went to the sides of his aching head in a futile attempt to press it back into shape. Only with the greatest effort did he manage to still the throbbing and examine the scene around him.

Forty-two half-breed warriors lay sprawled about him in various postures of drunken stupor. The five he had sent off to Haggard the previous night had not returned. By all the Spirits! They were to attack the town this morning!

Joe groaned at this realization. It only served to emphasize the incredible extent of his hangover. Rising like a cow, hind parts first, with his buttocks high in the air, and then pushing with his arms, Joe reached a vertical position. He swayed unsteadily and shambled across the sandy ground to a canteen. He tore at the stopper with trembling fingers and took in greedy gulps of tepid water. Then he bent forward and poured another large quantity over his pounding head. Partially recovered, he set about kicking awake several still-supine forms. They had to build a fire, cook a meal, and restore themselves enough to fight another battle.

Images of the previous day's slaughter filled Joe's mind and cheered him. It had been good. It would be better in Haggard. If nothing else, there would be more whiskey and women in the town. As the band of renegades began to stir, Joe searched about for a whiskey bottle that might contain at least a little something to make him well.

Charlie Roundtree sat on the ground a short distance from the wagon. About it lay women and young girls. As he studied them, regret began to steal over him. He should not be the one to take them to the camp. Yet, he could trust none of his drunken men to get them there.

Even so, he felt less than confident about Joe

187

Sureshot leading the attack on Haggard. For all of his abilities—like Charlie, he could read and write in English and had a quick grasp of military tactics—he had a weak side to his nature. He liked whiskey and women too much. There shouldn't be much resistance in Haggard. Although, as he well knew, even the least slip in planning could cause disaster. Would Joe remember everything he must do to insure success?

The call to individual glory sounded too easily in Joe's ears. For three years, from the age of thirteen to sixteen, Joe had ridden with Osage war parties. The hunger to count *coup* called to him like succulent flesh to a starving man. But all was in the hands of the spirits now, he thought as he rose from his contemplations and began to rouse the women.

"Get up. Get moving. Climb back in that wagon," he ordered. As he went among the reclining forms, he found himself constantly attracted to a plump little girl of four or five.

She had nearly translucent skin and a sweet smile. Her arms and legs, still chubby with baby fat, had a nice roundness, as did her face. She blinked big, frightened blue eyes at him and he smiled in return. Suddenly, he found himself salivating.

With the flow of liquid, other urges rose in him. Charlie walked over and took the girl in his arms. He carried her to where he had tethered his horse, already saddled for the journey. Swinging onto his mount, wordlessly he rode off into the brush, the trembling girl clutched to his chest.

188

Stunned beyond further complaint, the child's mother watched in wordless horror. In a languorous stupor, the women went about their morning needs, freshened themselves as best they could under their present conditions, and climbed aboard the wagon. There they sat patiently, waiting whatever fate decreed for them.

Half an hour passed. A stirring in the grass might have attracted the attention of some, though they never showed it. The rustling grew louder, and occurred in many places. Still the defeated women of Cimarron did not stir. A dozen men suddenly appeared, weapons in hand.

"O-Orville? Orville, is that you?" one matron inquired shakily.

"Yes, Millicent," Orville's quavery voice replied.

"Where is your escort, ladies?" Eli Holten inquired, his eyes constantly moving to take in the surroundings.

"He . . . he's gone. Took little Sarah Smith and rode off into the brush over there," another woman supplied.

More of the men from Cimarron came into view. As though released from a dread magician's spell, the women began to weep and cry out in relief at their deliverance. Overjoyed, they wailed and dashed about to embrace their own menfolk, then others of the liberators, especially the stern-looking scout.

When the jubilation had calmed a bit, Eli questioned the women further. "Which way did Roundtree go with the girl?"

189

They pointed in the same direction. "She . . . she's just a baby," the unfortunate Sarah's mother blubbered despondently.

"Detail four men to accompany the wagon back to Cimarron," Holten commanded. "The rest of you, retrieve the horses and make ready to head for Haggard. We should get there in time to catch the renegades in the rear."

A hearty cheer went up from the men. Relieved now that their women had been freed, they hungered for a big portion of revenge on the half-breed army.

"I should catch up with you within a half hour," Eli assured them. Leading Sonny, Holten went off after Charlie Roundtree.

Holten's search took most of the time he had allotted himself. After clearing the low screen of sage and Russian thistle, he swung into the saddle and urged Sonny along at a brisk walk. Despite his pace, twenty-five minutes had gone by before he came upon a makeshift camp. There a scene of absolute horror met his steely gray gaze.

The dismembered corpse of a small girl lay about the clearing. Some of her flesh, a chunk that could have been part buttock and a thigh, had been roasted over a fire just long enough for a crispy brown crust to form on its outer surface; then most of the flesh had been eaten with apparent gusto. Inured to nearly every act of savagery or grisly sight the wide-flung plains could conjure up, Holten's usual calm departed him. While he fumed in impotent anger, his stomach rebelled. Fighting the urge to vomit, Holten got down and studied the ground.

No wonder the Ponca tribesmen who visited Dodge City knew nothing of Charlie Roundtree. They did not visit with him because the renegade was not a Ponca. He was one of the degenerate Tonkawa, the only cannibals among all the Indian peoples of North America.

Their loathesome practices had isolated the Tonkawa tribe from all others, who held them in contempt, regarding them with disgust and hatred. Hunted down like the animals they were, by whites and red men alike, the tribe had become almost extinct. That beneficent circumstance, unfortunately, apparently did not apply to Charlie Roundtree.

This gruesome scene also explained the charred and gnawed human bones found earlier by the patrol. O'Kelly had been right. A stinking Tonk. Holten conquered his gorge long enough to gather and bury the pitiful remains of little Sarah Smith. He deemed it better to let her rest here, rather than subject her parents to the horror of how she had met her end. Unaccustomed to religious devotion, the scout felt a bit uncomfortable as he removed his hat and gazed upward.

"Lord," he began awkwardly. "This little girl didn't have long on this earth of ours. Now she's gone. I hope my Sioux brothers are wrong when they say that a person who is missing some parts, or has been torn to bits, can't enter whole into the next world. We can only hope Sarah Smith is back in one piece and in heaven with You. Uh . . . amen. And, Lord," he added as an afterthought, his anger rising again, "I promise to find Charlie Roundtree and make him pay. Slowly . . . and . . . painfully."

Two minutes later, Eli had returned to the saddle. A quick study of the ground and the tracks he found leading out indicated that Charlie must have heard the arrival of the rescue force and abandoned the women to save himself. His trail led roughly westward, toward Haggard.

Weary and sore, Susan Walters arrived in Dodge City in the early hours of the morning. She went directly to her small rented house. It sat squat and dark on a tiny plot of ground, behind its white picket fence. Seeing no sign of anyone about, she put the mule in the small stable behind the clapboard dwelling and entered through the rear door.

Funny, she thought as she crossed into the living room. From the tone of the note, she had expected to find Eli here. She lighted a lamp and examined her surroundings.

Nothing had been disturbed. Yet she sensed an alien presence . . . as though someone lurked beyond the partly open bedroom door. Or . . . *had* waited there, patiently, like a spider endlessly spinning a web, its mind filled with the juicy prey it expected to entrap. A shudder coursed through her body and Susan chided herself for being frivolous and imaginative. She had no food, of course, but a tin of Arbuckle's rested on a lower cabinet shelf in the kitchen. She kindled a fire and

192

set a pot to boiling. Where was Eli?

When it came, that expected knock, Susan had begun to pour a cup of coffee. The jarring sound, long anticipated, caused her to give a start. Scalding coffee splashed over the rim of the cup and spread, steaming, across the table. Quickly she set the pot aside and rushed to the front of the house.

Why had Eli insisted on such secrecy, she wondered as she threw the door open to . . .

Hiram Skaggs stood smiling confidently on the small stoop. At once, Susan started to slam the door, but the banker raised a hand in a preemptive gesture.

"Please, Miss Susan," he began in a tone unfamiliar to her. "I have information of importance to you."

"What could that possibly be?" Susan snapped impatiently.

"I . . . I've heard from Eli Holten. He contacted me with some information vitally important at this time." Skaggs paused and looked around as though fearful of being overheard. "May I come in? This is a highly confidential matter."

"Uh . . . I . . . are you sure Eli sent *you* to me?"

"Your friend, the scout, said that what he had to say he could entrust to no one but you."

Susan took an unsure, hesitant step backward and the pudgy banker bustled through the space that opened up. Inside the living room, he removed his hat and glanced around, a small smile of triumph hidden behind one hand.

"Now, what is this all about, Mister Skaggs?"

"The safety of the entire community is at stake," Skaggs told her dramatically. "I dare say, the whole country. The information must reach the Army through other than normal channels. Holten said to contact a, ah, General . . ."

"Corrington?"

"Yes, that's it. He said that someone high up in the Army was in league with the renegades. He said that you must get that to General Corrington."

Suspicious, Susan questioned the banker closely. "How is it that Eli chose to come to you?"

Skaggs preened himself. "Well, my dear, I hardly have a reputation for being a stalwart advocate for the Army, but I must admit, I've been mistaken about Holten all along. He is a conscientious and patriotic young man. He did not simply walk off, leaving his responsibilities behind and you with a broken heart. He was abducted. Taken by the very men who murdered your husband and perpetrated those despicable raids against the homesteaders."

"Wha . . . Why? How do you know this?"

"Because he escaped. At least for the time being. But he has to keep on the move. He knows the identity of the officer who has been helping the renegades. That man is aware that Holten has seen through his nefarious scheme. To come out in the open would be to invite his own death. That is why we must be, ah, discreet. After you have an opportunity to rest and refresh yourself, come by my house and I'll give you the papers Holten left for you. They identify the Judas and give all the particulars."

"Why not at your office?"

"We must be most careful that no one knows that we have anything to do with this. The renegades have eyes everywhere. So does the traitor. For now, let me bid you an early good morning. I will be on my way. Don't forget. My house later today. It's two blocks over, in between the one with the gingerbread woodwork and the Morton house."

"All right. I'll be there after I get some sleep."

"We've been through the drill twice now without any errors," Lieutenant Stone told the mayor of Haggard. "Everyone knows what part to play. Now all we have to do is wait for the renegades."

"Are . . . are you absolutely certain this will work?"

"As sure as anyone can be about a battle yet unfought. There's a gamble in anything, Mister Mayor. But this plan was thought out by my scout, Eli Holten, an expert on Plains Indian tribes and their fighting styles. Modesty aside, I provided certain touches that allow for the half-breeds' adaptation of military tactics. *We* know our trade—better, I feel confident, than the followers of Charlie Roundtree. Now we have to put everything back in place and wait for the arrival of the enemy. Remember, it must appear that you are all in a total panic, that everyone is packing up to move out. Like it did when we arrived early last night.''

The mayor glowered at this reminder of the community's shared cowardice. "I'll hold you personally responsible for the success of this mad enterprise, Lieutenant Stone. If these marauders descry your ruse and penetrate the defenses, we will all be murdered in our homes.''

"It won't get that far, Mayor. Believe me. When the renegades are fully committed and meet our strong resistance, they will be hit in the rear by the men from Cimarron. That way we will be able to crush them easily.''

"I can only pray that you are right, Lieutenant."

"So do I, sir.''

Chapter Sixteen

Two hours after the sun heaved itself over the long, flat horizon of the Kansas prairie, the first of the mixed-bloods began to amble into Haggard. They came singly and in pairs. Joe Sureshot had chosen to follow the plan laid out by Charlie Roundtree for Cimarron. Everything seemed peaceful enough. It looked as though a lot of the locals planned to get out of town. Word of the earlier raid must have reached here soon after.

"Easier to haul it all off if it's already in wagons," one renegade remarked to his companion.

Within a half hour, a dozen men had entered town, spacing themselves along the main thoroughfare in position to strike at the unsuspecting yokels. Two of them lounged at the tie rail in front of the saloon as a bowlegged old woman and her grandson shuffled past.

Sgt. Clerance O'Kelly peeked out from under his blue checkered sun bonnet. Had his expression been clearly visible to the two half-breeds at the tie rail it would have certainly disconcerted them. A brave young boy held the soldier's gnarled hand as they ambled along the wooden walkway. Approaching them from the opposite direction came a young man, awkward in his unfamiliar civilian suit.

In accordance with Eli Holten's plan and the cavalry noncom's instructions, the infantrymen had stripped themselves of their uniforms and now appeared on the streets acting as if they were fleeing civilians. More of their number and most of the people of Haggard, hid in the second stories of the buildings along Main Street, waiting for the attack to begin. O'Kelly and the fearless lad rounded the corner into a narrow side street.

Part way along, he saw two more of the raiders. One of the pair stepped onto the boardwalk and peered through the bars of a tiny window at the interior of the small jail. Within he saw two of his comrades, sent in the night before to reconnoiter. They lay asleep on straw-stuffed mattresses. Obviously they had been arrested. Probably for being drunk. Nothing unusual there, the half-breed thought to himself. All they needed was the signal to start the takeover.

Only one man had been detailed to handle the livery. He wondered when no one came out to greet him, but thought it of little importance. After a few minutes, he swung out of the saddle and walked into the cool, darkened interior of the stable.

Greater darkness awaited him as a ten-pound sledge, wielded by the willing hands of a private in Company K, Fourth United States Infantry, smashed into the back of his head. The heavy hammer shattered the murdering breed's skull and sent a shower of blood and fluid flying through the stalls. Two horses whickered uneasily at the smell of the gore.

Back at the jail, the renegade turned away from the window to inform his friend of what he saw, only to see the man sprawled in the filth of the street, a trickle of blood coming from a deep cut in his scalp. He also saw a .32 Whitneyville Armory revolver in the small hand of a young boy. Before he could laugh at this puny threat, Hellfire erupted in his head and he crashed to the plankwalk, his eyes rolled far up in their sockets.

"Two more o' the bastards outta the way," Clerance O'Kelly remarked as he put away his Schofield .45 in the beaded string purse he carried.

"Yeah," the freckle-faced boy breathed out in awe, his eyes wide and dancing with the light of excitement.

"I think we oughtta take a mosey over ta the gen'ril store."

One by one the infiltrators met with similar, silent accidents that eliminated them from the contest. At the general mercantile, O'Kelly arrived in time to find a half-breed behind that establishment bent over in the act of setting it afire. The unsuspecting raider's skull made a musical *bonk* when O'Kelly clobbered him with a stout piece of firewood. That clout seemed to put a stop to the idea of arson.

"There's another one around here," the boy who accompanied Sergeant O'Kelly hissed at him.

"Why didn't you do something about it?"

"I did. He was takin' a leak and I kicked him in the balls."

O'Kelly found the marauder on the ground, doubled up in a puddle of his own urine and gasping breathlessly while he clutched his aching parts. O'Kelly pulled the breed's knife and, adding insult to injury, slashed the hostile's throat. Quickly he ran toward the front of the building to locate Lieutenant Stone.

"We gotta get some sort of fire going to signal the others to ride in, Lieutenant."

"That's already being taken care of, Sergeant O'Kelly. Three of the men are setting fire to a barrel of oily blankets and rags down by the livery. There will also be smoke from behind the mercantile."

"I hope it wasn't bein' set by a couple o' our side who happen to be a bit on the dark side."

"No, Sergeant. Why do you ask?"

"The lad an' me just clobbered a pair like that."

Despite the strain of this carefully choreographed battle, Lieutenant Richard Stone found time to laugh. "Carry on, Sergeant," he managed to get out through his mirth.

Within another ten minutes, all of the covert attackers had been taken out of action. By then, billows of smoke rose above the buildings of the town and soldiers designated to play an important role because of their loud voices, began to cry "Fire!"

The signal worked.

From outside Haggard, the clear notes of a bugle sounded and the remaining raiders thundered into town.

Too late Joe Sureshot saw that it was not the livery burning so smokily, but a barrel of refuse before its door. He also spotted the corral full of Army mules. The soldiers had arrived ahead of him and this had to be some sort of trap.

Then the wagons began to move. Quickly the barricades went into place, as had been rehearsed the night before. Wagons and buggies blocked alleys and streets, not to keep the hostiles out, but to thoroughly trap them inside the town.

Confined to the main street, the outlaw half-breeds could only mill about in confusion. Yellow-orange blossomed from the muzzles of rifles that poked out from every hole, window, and door crack in the walls of the town.

Reluctant to do so, Susan nevertheless went to Hiram Skaggs's home at eight in the morning. He greeted her warmly enough and showed her into an austere parlor that contained little other than functional furniture.

"Thank you for coming, Miss Susan. Please take a seat and I'll bring us coffee."

"You needn't bother, Mister Skaggs," Susan replied, her voice tight with apprehension.

"Oh, it's no bother at all." The banker departed, to return a few minutes later with a silver serving tray, cups, saucers, and all the accoutrements.

"Now, what is this about Eli being taken by the renegades?" Susan demanded as Skaggs began to pour.

"That's what he told me," Skaggs responded. "Some of them jumped him here in Dodge and carried him off to a camp they maintain. He managed to escape, but knows they followed. He also suspects that they have notified their confidant in the Army at Fort Dodge."

"I . . . see. Then he is still in great danger?"

"I would presume so. Drink your coffee, my dear."

Obediently, Susan took a long sip. It tasted slightly bitter, but she discounted that as the product of bachelor cooking.

"What about the statements you mentioned last night?"

"Ah, yes. I'll get them for you."

After Skaggs left the room, Susan felt for a moment as though the walls writhed and undulated. She blinked and helped herself to more coffee. It seemed an eternity before the banker returned. Involuntarily, Susan yawned. She patted daintily at her lips and batted her eyes again. She found it quite difficult to raise her eyelids. For the first time, since he had called on her during the night, Susan noticed that Hiram Skaggs was smiling.

Roundtree left a clear enough trail. It led directly to Haggard. As Eli Holten rode nearer, he could clearly hear the sound of gunfire. Charlie Roundtree had made it in time for the main charge, the scout surmised when he came within sight of the town and saw its traplike defenses all in place. Off to one side he caught sight of the volunteers from Cimarron and swung Sonny in that direction. One of the men raised his Winchester above his head in greeting.

"We wondered if you would make it, Holten," he called out as the scout reined in.

"We're all here, that's what matters," Eli told him. "Head around to the far side of town. Some of the soldiers will be waiting to let us in."

Within minutes, the fresh fighting men entered Haggard. At first, Charlie's murderous gang hardly noticed them. Too busy with trying to keep alive, the increased volume of fire had little meaning to them. Then the renegade on Charlie's left took flight. A column of buckshot, fired by an angry, mounted farmer from Cimarron, splashed the half-breed's back into an ugly red pulp and carried him over his horse's head. Startled, Charlie looked around to find his formerly well-disciplined force under attack from yet another direction.

"Bugler, sound 'Recall'!" Charlie shouted. To

203

those closest to him, he confided. "We're out-numbered. We have to form a wedge and fight our way out of town."

A shower of sprightly notes fractured the smoke-filled air. The renegades who could still move began to form up as Charlie directed. The concentrated volume of their fire forced the defenders to take shelter momentarily. That gave Charlie the break he needed. With a proper cavalry arm signal, he waved his troops forward.

They charged not away from, but toward the newly arrived civilian volunteers.

Caught off guard, some of the farmers and shopkeepers panicked and spurred their horses into side streets. Others bolted out of the way or dismounted in an attempt to avoid certain death.

"Hold fast!" Holten uselessly shouted at them.

Unaccustomed to combat for the most part, the sodbusters and store clerks sought only to save their own lives. Charlie Roundtree and his men thundered along the main street, under only desultory fire.

"Burn the town," Charlie shouted.

Once free of the closing ring of blazing weapons, the renegades spread out and began to do their leader's bidding. Flames began to lick at several structures and the individual breeds took time to aim carefully and pick off some of the snipers on the roofs of buildings.

Lieutenant Stone quickly evaluated the situation and made a decision. "Form the men up, Sergeant. Fix bayonets and we'll charge them."

Sergeant O'Kelly arranged the men in three

ranks that extended the width of the street. At his command the familiar metallic clatter that attended the attaching of bayonets to Springfield rifles was heard. Lieutenant Stone stepped in front of his men, revolver in one hand, saber in the other.

"At my command, the first rank will kneel, second assume the offhand position. Third rank will take a half-step to the right and do the same. We will fire a volley, advance the third rank through and fire again, then charge with cold steel. Follow me, men!"

Expecting only to encounter frightened townspeople and incompetent farmers, Charlie Roundtree and his renegades had not been prepared for the awesome sight of an infantry bayonet charge. Several stopped to gape, eyes wide, jaws sagging, as the soldiers advanced along the main street. The blue-uniformed man out front stepped to one side as the troops halted. He raised his saber and shouted a command.

The front rank went to their knees and placed rifle butts to their shoulders. Behind them, the second and third ranks shifted their positions and took deadly aim.

"Fire!" Lieutenant Stone bellowed.

A curtain of greasy powder smoke covered the soldiers as they executed their next evolution, which brought the third file forward to kneel while all reloaded. Then, spaced sufficiently apart to allow each man a good field of fire, they opened up again.

Renegades fell here and there, though the main

force did not break.

Stone's action gave Eli Holten a chance to rally his small contingent. Swiftly they rode down on the surprised breeds, weapons flashing fire and smoke. Holten's aim proved every bit as good as his bravado. Six of the would-be warriors toppled from their horses as he closed in. Then a screeching shout came from the soldiers.

"Chaa-rrrge!" Lieutenant Stone howled.

His men rose as one and ran toward the disorganized enemy. Midmorning sunlight glinted off the long, murderous blades of their bayonets.

Two half-breeds got skewered like suckling pigs before the renegade army overcame their shock at a combined attack by infantry and cavalry. Another died shrieking before Charlie Roundtree managed to galvanize his men into a cohesive force once more. Held together by the mixed-blood leader's iron will, they goaded their horses into a gallop and headed out of town, firing randomly behind them in an attempt to gain precious seconds.

Lt. Richard Stone emptied his Schofield at point-blank range into a cluster of stragglers and hacked another down with his saber. Abruptly, he dropped his weapons, took two staggering steps and fell to the ground.

Susan awakened with a stinging start. A smart, loud smack on her bare rump had jolted her into consciousness. She lay on her stomach. Her first, tentative movement made her aware of the tightness of the bonds that restrained her, legs spread wide apart. She struggled feebly against them. She wanted to cry out, but her mouth had been efficiently gagged. A dull ache rose from her groin. Where was she?

A wild, disoriented look around identified the room as one long abandoned. Dusty, with cobwebs hanging from corners, its windows smeared to opaqueness, the only familiar sight she could focus on was the red brick outer wall. She must be upstairs in the bank building, Susan decided. But how . . . and why?

The answer came unpleasantly. Hiram Skaggs, entirely naked, his flabby body fish-belly white, stepped around into her sight. A greasy grin spread his unnaturally bluish lips.

"Well, my dear. I must say I have enjoyed my first excursion. Not as jolly as I'm sure the future ones will be. Oh . . . I see from your eyes you want to know what I mean. Simple, really. While you were unconscious from the powder I put in your coffee, I managed to relieve the pressure on my magic wand in that sweet cavern of yours. Now that you've come around, I can begin to teach you what a real man can do. No more of this ball-less scout for you."

Skaggs cocked his head to one side and pursed his lips as though listening to a difficult question. A thin dart of pink tongue came into view and flicked, serpentlike, across his lips. "You want to know where you are . . . and why I'm doing this. Again, not difficult to answer. You're in an unused storeroom above my bank. As to why, it's because I've lusted after you since the first time I saw you.

"Such a pity you chose to reject my well-meaning advances, dear Susan. We could have been much more compatible without the need of these unsightly fetters. Ah, but now, I feel a certain demanding rigidity returning. I think I shall indulge myself a bit more. Such lovely flesh you have, my dear . . ."

Chapter Seventeen

In Haggard, the battle seemed somehow incomplete. Although renegade bodies were strewn about the town, the prairie community continued to burn. Eli Holten made a quick count and determined that more than half of Charlie Roundtree's half-breed army had managed to escape.

"A cool-headed one, that Roundtree," Holten remarked to one of the soldiers who accompanied him around the scene of conflict.

"Yes, sir. He must have been in the Army for some time. Knew all the right commands and when to use them."

"You saw that, too, eh?"

Sergeant O'Kelly hurried up to where the scout stood. "Beggin' yer pardon, Mister Holten. Lieutenant Stone is mortally wounded, I fear. He's lyin' over yonder with a bullet in his chest."

"Take me to him."

"Right away, Mister Holten, sir."

Lt. Richard Stone lay with his head propped on a rolled blanket. His face had lost all color and was taking on the waxy aspect of a corpse. His eyes, however, glowed with an inner fire that might indicate a determination to live or be a harbinger of death. He tried to rise when Holten approached, only to fall back, gasping weakly.

"Y-you have to pursue them," Stone gurgled through the blood accumulating in his right lung. "You h-have to run those renegade bastards to the ground."

"I'll leave right away," Holten told him.

"N-not just you. Th-the whole platoon's got to go. Too many of them. The breeds' mounts must be near to exhaustion by now. Th-those mules of ours are hardy, if nothing else. They c-can give you an edge. Take the men and ride, Holten. I . . . I'm done for."

Eli looked to Sgt. Clerance O'Kelly, who still wore the bonnet and skirts of his disguise. "You're second in command, O'Kelly. It's up to you to do what the Lieutenant wants."

"Not me, sir. I'm a good noncom. Truth to tell, there ain't many better'n me, 'cept of course First Soldier, O'Brannigan. But what we need is an officer in command. Bein' as how yer position as a chief scout is the same as a major's—"

"Oh, no, Sergeant. Why, I don't even think it would be legal."

Many of the soldiers had gathered around their

fallen leader and looked on with silent interest at this exchange. O'Kelly turned to appeal to them.

"What d'ye say, lads? Would ye be wantin' to go after them what done in the good lieutenant?"

Shouts of "Yes!" and "Damned right!" filled the air.

"An' would ye be favorin' Mister Holten here to be leadin' us?"

Out of uniform, the soldiers took a decidedly unmilitary view of events. Like any group of civilians, they determined to take a vote on it. With unanimous approval, they elected Eli Holten to the position of leadership.

"Your Colonel Waterstratt will have a full-sized fit over this," Eli cautioned.

"At least I won't be there to hear him," Lieutenant Stone managed between bouts of coughing and spitting up blood. "Good luck . . . Eli."

"Good luck to you, Rick."

Stone managed a smile. "Where I'm going, luck'll have little to do with it."

Already, O'Kelly had started to round up the infantrymen and get them to the livery corral to saddle their mules. As the work progressed Eli and O'Kelly held a council of war.

"We have the upper hand now. Roundtree has lost enough men so that we outnumber him. I figure he'll head for his camp. And I know where that is. Within about three hours we should be ready to wipe them out to the last man."

*   *   *

By midafternoon, Susan's lovely body had been marked by angry red stripes and ugly, puckered welts. Behind her gag she sobbed with frustration and humiliation at the suffering she had been forced to endure at the hands of such a twisted monster as Hiram Skaggs. Several times during the day he had left her to take care of business.

Naked, cold, and alone in the dingy room, she had repeatedly tested her bonds to determine if they could be loosened. Always her efforts ended in disappointment. And always, Skaggs returned to inflict more pain and degradation on her.

At last he came back, a smile of satisfaction on his face instead of his usual mask of lust. The late afternoon sun slanted milkily through one window and he rubbed his hands gleefully.

"We're extending the usual business hours," he told her in a chatty, conversational way. "The raid on Cimarron has started a regular run of farmers wanting to sell out. I'm only too glad to accommodate them, naturally. At . . . a penny on the dollar now. All that remains to be done is to see that the raids stop. Then . . . oh, then, Susan my dear, I will be a very, very rich man." Skaggs clapped his hands together in utter delight.

"Are we comfortable on that old desk? Good. You know, Susan, you're not too bad in the bed department. Nice and tight. How would you like to spend your days with me, as a wealthy woman in California?"

Far to the southwest, high in the stratosphere,

huge, billowing collections of moisture combined to give birth to a towering mushroom-shaped cloud. Black on its underside, roiling with internal turmoil, it soon spawned ominous like-nesses. This brewing storm sent outriders scud-ding across the Kansas sky, darkening the day and bringing chill winds to buffet man, beast, and plant.

"Sure an' there's one hell of a storm comin' up," Clerance O'Kelly remarked to Eli Holten.

"If it's anything like Dakota, we could be hock-deep in mud in half an hour."

"Ah, now ye've got the right o' it. Far once I bless these mules we're burdened with. They can slog through mire that would put any horse belly up. Exceptin' yer own fine mount, that is."

"Sonny's sturdy enough, though I wouldn't want to press him in a real goose drowner."

Still, Holten wanted to push on, even when the heavens opened and the first skirmish of cold sheets of rain pelted the pursuing white men. Eli knew this assault was a light one compared to what could be expected from the angry, churning clouds that hovered over them.

"Mister Holten. Somethin' up ahead," the point man shouted as he galloped back to the column.

"What is it?"

"Dead half-breeds. You'll have to see it to believe it."

A few minutes later, the soldiers came upon the grisly scene.

Seven dead renegades lay sprawled amidst the sagebrush and cacti. All had been scalped. Weap-

213

ons and valuables had been stripped from their bodies.

"Apparently there is some dissension in the ranks, Sergeant," Eli remarked drily.

"Aye. The heathen devils is fightin' among themselves they are."

A quick examination of the corpses produced no sign of Charlie Roundtree. For a moment, the rain slackened and Holten studied the ground more carefully.

"Roundtree must still be in charge," he opined to the attentive O'Kelly. "He probably finished off some of these himself. Keep order in the ranks."

"Bloody savage."

"Look here. They left in two groups. Only a few tracks continue on toward the Arkansas River. The rest are making a big swing."

"It could be an old Injun trick," O'Kelly suggested.

"No. See the depth of those hoofprints? Even with the rain they're pronounced. Those horses are carrying weight all right. Could it be that they are headed back toward Cimarron or Haggard to stage a second attack?"

"Heaven forbid, sir."

"We'll have to check it out to be certain."

From his hiding place on the back slope of a slight rise, some two hundred yards away, Joe Sureshot watched the white soldiers go over the ground around the site of the killings. A smile brightened his dark features when the men mounted up and started to follow the trail of the more numerous tracks that swung back in the general direction from which they had come. He rose and rejoined his mountless companions.

"It's all right," Joe told them. "The white soldiers have fallen for Charlie's trick. They follow the horses with rocks in the sacks on their backs."

Slowly the column began to slog through the thickening mud. They followed a shallow ravine for some distance. Although to do so entailed a considerable risk because the rain was getting heavier, this course took them quickly away from the enemy. When at last they stopped to climb clear of the dry creek bed, the renegades knew they had won.

Billy Iron Hand had only sixteen summers. It had puffed his chest with pride to be chosen by Charlie Roundtree to follow the white soldiers and make certain they remained fooled by the ruse that lured them back toward the towns of Cimarron and Haggard. Now Billy shivered slightly. His clothes were already sodden and still more rain fell from the sky. The clouds had darkened and a sharp wind blew out of the southwest. Lightning flashed all around and rolling booms of thunder muttered ominously. A bigger mass of black thunderheads was following on the heels of this light storm. The rain was a good omen, though, Billy knew.

Any trail left by the decoy horses had been washed out. Only an occasional string of droppings gave any indication that the animals had passed this way. The farther they go, Billy thought, the better. It might not be raining ahead. If not, any trail that became visible would still lead the soldiers astray. Several of Charlie's renegades were driving the rock-laden mounts toward the farming communities. Until visual contact was made, the whites would follow along ignorantly. Every possibility had been accounted for.

If the whites did swerve away from Cimarron, Billy had been charged to ride swiftly back to camp and warn Charlie Roundtree. The leader's plan could not fail. Confidently, Billy urged his pony closer and, for a distraction, counted the number of soldiers once more.

Suddenly Billy realized something was wrong. His count didn't come out right. Someone was missing. Carefully he accounted for the mule-borne troops, their sergeants and . . . That was it!

The one Charlie had called Holten no longer rode out front, leading the men along the faint traces of trail, like a scout should. Perhaps he had ridden ahead. If he'd seen the herd of riderless horses, he would know they had been duped. The young half-breed began to move out to get ahead of the white men. As the gulley in which he had hidden himself narrowed, Billy Iron Hand dismounted to lead his horse back onto the flat prairie so he could gallop away.

A sixth sense made him tense as he went about the task of coaxing the nervous animal up the

216

crumbling sand and loam embankment. Lightning crashed near by, momentarily blinding him, and the roar of thunder deafened the boy. A small cottonwood tree ignited from a direct strike. Once more a jangle of warning shot through Billy's body. He turned to look around—only to see a rifle butt headed toward his skull.

Chapter Eighteen

Breathlessly, the half-breeds with Joe Sureshot
stumbled into camp. They had run for better than
three miles in the unceasing rain. Charlie Roundtree sat glowering in his lodge. He had waited
until the majority of his force returned. Without
comment he walked out among them and called
for the young men and boys who had guarded the
camp during the renegade army's absence.

"All of you line up over there," he commanded.

When they'd obeyed, Charlie stalked along
in front of them, lips curled in an angry snarl.
More than a few had wounds, though this did not
affect the outcome Charlie had already decided
upon.

"All of you listen to me. We lost the fight at

Haggard because these ignorant puppies let the scout, Holten, escape. They are not fit to be part of our mighty army. Those who failed at their posts must be punished. That is my decision."

Coolly, Charlie drew two revolvers and shot every tenth man among the surviving guards. The other men blanched at the severity of their leader's retribution. Once the decimation had been completed and fresh rounds had been inserted in the chambers of Charlie's six-guns, he faced the assembled renegades.

"These are not alone in deserving punishment. We did not defeat the soldiers and people of Haggard because of the scout, but also because many among you failed to keep your discipline in the face of a superior force." He gestured to the corpses.

"Observe the demands of discipline. I will not cut you down where you stand, though many of you deserve it. Already seven of you have died by my hand because of their cowardice. In doing so, they also helped fool the whites into thinking we have come apart as a sound military organization. In that they are wrong! We are as strong as ever! The battle went against us, but we're far from being lost. In fact, we have come much closer to our goal," Charlie told them. "Cimarron and Haggard are burning. The people are frightened. Soon they will leave in droves. When that time comes, *we* will own the land, and *we* will own the supplies that will be sold to those we allow to work our land for us, taking only a small portion as their due.

"The day will come when the whites return in such numbers that we will be forced to sell the land again. But until then, it is ours, and we will be able to put a few whites to working it like slaves."

A loud cheer went up. All about the camp dogs howled and yipped. While Charlie ranted on, Eli Holten scooted through the drizzle, coming closer and closer to the edge of the camp in the big bend of the Arkansas. Although several mutts had detected him, the dogs had been set to baying by the executions and the scent of blood so no one paid him any mind. Carefully the scout took stock of what had been happening.

More bodies.

An idea dawned on the scout, one both simple and grim in its import. It was not dissension that was leaving so many half-breed bodies lying around. Quite the contrary, Holten realized. Charlie Roundtree, aping the stringent discipline of the Army in times past, had gone back even further to the olden days of the Romans, who'd invented the idea of decimation as a suitable punishment.

If a unit of soldiers had not lived up to their Roman leaders' expectations, the scout recalled, every tenth man was executed. So it must be in Roundtree's camp. The horrible excesses that the fanatic half-breed had gone to in order to enforce discipline and control left a hollow, sick feeling in the pit of Eli's stomach. Stealthily he withdrew from the enbankment overlooking the camp.

He followed a different path to where he'd tethered Sonny and swung wearily into the saddle. He had been nearly forty hours without sleep, had eaten only scant snatches of jerky and cold beans, and the storm had taxed him and his mount even further. Head hanging, Holten rode back to where the soldiers and a handful of civilian volunteers from Cimarron and Haggard waited.

"Are they there, then?" O'Kelly inquired in a lowered voice.

"Yes. Roundtree and most of his men. He shot a lot of them for disobedience. The rest are fixing what meals they can."

"I could go for a little somethin' meself. Me innards are convinced me mouth's gone on a long furlough."

"After we deal with Roundtree," Eli cautioned.

"An' this forever, bleedin' rain quits. Tell me, what was it made you suspicious about the trail that was leadin' us back toward the towns?"

Eli thought for a moment. "Honestly, I can't say exactly, O'Kelly. From the start I wasn't sure what we thought we saw, in fact, had happened. Then, when we came on more tracks, the horses seemed to be bunched up a bit too much. Riders would probably not be so close together, unless they had a lot of wounded to care for. Herded horses would be contained in a tight surround by the men driving them for easier manageability. Particularly with this storm going on. Then, when I came across the boy watching us, I knew the horses were decoys."

"Sure an' we all could by then. What now?"

"We get a little rest, let the renegades calm down some, then we hit them with all we've got."

Lt. Col. Lemuel Waterstratt sat behind his desk at Fort Dodge and looked disconsolately at the nasty weather outside. Young Stone's patrol had been out entirely too long without sending in a report. On the colonel's desk lay a sheet of paper informing him of the massacre at Cimarron. Where the hell had Stone been?

Much more of that and people would begin to believe that blowhard, Skaggs. He wondered what the army-hating buffoon was up to at that moment. Probably making money hand over fist as the farmers and their families panicked and rushed to sell out. The more he thought of Skaggs, the more the colonel felt that he should know the fat banker from somewhere in the past. Surely he would remember anyone who loathed the Army so. But try as he might, he could never make a connection.

At least there was one bright spot to improve his otherwise miserable day. The patrols sent out to the western border of the state would be returning the day after next. With cavalry once again at hand, short work could be made of these rene-gades. All the colonel could do was wait.

Squealing like a rutting boar, Hiram Skaggs

thumped mightily into Susan's sore and reddened orifice. He had untied her, turned the helpless young woman over, and bent her backward across the low desk. Her ankles he had spread apart and secured to the legs of one side, while her arms had been bound to those of the other. He had so positioned her that her aching, dripping parts rested within a fraction of an inch of the edge. Then he had entered her roughly, time and again.

Her strength had been greatly diminished during this long ordeal. Yet, the least taxing part had been Skaggs's repeated rapes. The man must need a tweezer, she thought, to find his organ when it is slack. He barely made a dent inside her ravaged passage. Even so, she was hungry, humiliated, cold, sweaty, and in pain. Although she felt dirty and shamefully used, she had hardly been worn out by Skaggs's deficient manhood. It was what he did during or after his frequent penetrations, when he tormented her with burning cigar tips and repeated applications of a riding crop, that hurt her and depleted her.

At least this time she had so far been spared that, for which Susan thanked heaven. Skaggs began to grunt and tremble as his time approached. With a mighty heave, he thrust his minimast as far as it would go inside her tender, nearly virginal body. His buttocks quivered and flexed, and she felt a hot spurt that fed her disgust. Somehow, someway—she kept this belief alive—Eli would find her and free her from this insatiable fiend.

Skaggs seemed to sense her thoughts, and driven

223

frantic by the discovery that hope remained alive within her, he began to punch and pummel her tightly stretched abdomen. Thank goodness, Susan thought wildly during this abuse. If he's put a baby in there, it will never survive this sort of treatment. She had to endure, had to hold on. She wanted to live. Silently, Susan kept repeating these thoughts as Skaggs grunted with the effort of hitting her. So long as she didn't beg for death, she knew Skaggs would keep her alive.

Although relatively unfamiliar with worldly things, Susan sensed that Skaggs would not enjoy killing her unless he knew first that he had broken her and made her a hopeless wretch.

"Beg me, you bitch!" he'd panted out. "Beg me to stop ripping you apart inside. Cry out to die, slut!"

With the coming of early evening and the departure of most of the downtown denizens, Skaggs removed Susan's gag. Only the two of them remained in the bank building. Skaggs had even sent home his usual night watchman. Slowly now, Susan worked her lips industriously to accumulate moisture in her mouth. Then she raised her head and smiled invitingly at the enraged banker.

"Come on, say it. Beg me not to kill you."

The slimy gobbet of spit hit Skaggs full in the face. As it ran down over the bridge of his nose and trailed across one cheek, he stared in disbelief at his victim.

"You'd better stick to chickens and ducks, Hiram-baby," Susan said in her nastiest voice, though the words felt dirty and alien in her mouth.

"They're more your size. Hurt me? You can't even tickle me. My Eli's got more head on his pecker than you have pecker. Why, I've seen little boys of eight who are hung better than you are."

"Pig, whore, dog, cunt!" Hiram Skaggs raged. Once more he began to pummel her until Susan fell into unconsciousness.

Chapter Nineteen

After the punitive slaughter, Charlie Roundtree declared a feast for the survivors. He ordered whiskey to be broken out, also sugar, coffee, and other treats. A cow, stolen on a previous farm raid, was brought forth, killed, and set to roasting over a blazing fire. The men whooped and hollered, and engaged in gambling, wrestling, and bragging about their fighting ability. Some took the time to wash themselves in the cool waters of the Arkansas River, while others sought out any available women and eased their tensions in that manner. Once the celebration got solidly under way, Joe Sureshot came to where Charlie Roundtree sat presiding over the festivities.

"The rain has ended, but we will have more by

morning. Even so, the soldiers are sure to come now," the half-breed lieutenant observed. "Not just those who ride mules. The cavalry will be after us soon."

"Yes. I know this and it troubles me."

"What will we do with all of . . . this?" Joe swung an arm to include the wagonloads and mounds of loot they had accumulated.

"It must be taken away. Tomorrow, when the storm can wash out our tracks. Down into Indian Territory. We can find caves where we can hide it safely in the Cookson Hills country. Then, when the time is right, we will bring it back."

With unusually clear insight, Joe inquired sourly, "Will the time ever be right?"

Three miles away from the Arkansas, in a shallow depression in the prairie, the mule-borne infantry and the civilian volunteers gathered to discuss the situation. Two of the more adept residents of Cimarron and the platoon's noncoms met with Eli Holten.

"Their only real means of escape is to cross the river or go to the west," Eli told the gathering. "A handful of sharpshooters on the bluffs will prevent any breakout to the north. The same for the narrow strip of sandy shore that follows the river eastward."

"We deny them any choice of terrain and we have them boxed up," one civilian commented.

"Exactly. You seem to have a fair grasp of

227

tactics, Mister Powers," Eli replied.

"I fought in the war," Powers answered sparingly.

"Good. Since this is to be a night attack, and I'm the only one who knows the ground inside camp, I'll have to lead the detail that goes in to eliminate the leaders. If you would, Powers, I'd like to put you in charge of the volunteers. Sergeant O'Kelly will command the infantry."

Clerance O'Kelly looked disappointed. "Sure an' I figgered to go in among the heathens with ye, Mister Holten."

"Not this time, O'Kelly. I'll have four men with me. Each of us is to eliminate one target. When the shooting starts, the mounted force is to sweep in from the west, closing off all escape, except across the river. We will fire as many lodges as we can to provide illumination. That's when the sharpshooters are to open up. We should be in and out in ten minutes. Any questions?"

"How many on our side do you expect we'll lose?" Orme, the second civilian inquired.

"Not many. The renegades are bone tired. By the time we move in, they will be drunk, full of food, and sound asleep. Our main job will be to force them to surrender, then to disarm them and round them up. Once the leaders are eliminated, the job should be simple.

"You all saw what happened when they got taken by surprise in Haggard. Without someone to think for them, they'll revert to individual fighting styles or plain give up. Either way, it should make our job easier."

"When do we do it?" Sergeant Wilson asked.

"We'll start off from here at midnight. Everyone should be in position by two in the morning. It looks like it'll be raining again by then. The storm should cover our approach. We'll figure the attack to start at two-thirty. By then the renegades should be sound asleep."

Burnthand Parrish scowled into the darkness and drizzle. His bushy black brows and overlarge eyes constituted the most prominent features on his face. He could have sworn he'd heard noises a bit ago. It could have been owls flittering in the trees, or rain wetting down a branch until it cracked. It could have been the soldiers who hunted them, he added uncomfortably. Why had he been put on this late guard duty? This had to be more of Charlie's idea of punishment. He had been one of the lucky ones to survive the execution of the younger sentries.

He couldn't even ride, but had to walk from one point to the other. Worse, he was sopping wet already and the rolling grumble of thunder sounded in the southwest. From time to time he saw flashes of lightning flickering on the horizon. Each flare came closer. The rifle felt heavy in his hands and his eyelids drooped. Not until an hour before sunrise would he be relieved. There! The noise had come again. Burnthand tried to detect some substance in the darkness that surrounded him. Again he failed to discern any threatening presence. He stifled a yawn and produced a rib bone from the roasted cow. At least, he could munch on that while he watched the sleeping camp.

Burnthand Parrish died in midbite.

Eli Holten and the four men he had picked slipped silently along the sandy bank of the Arkansas River. They had removed their hats to make them less distinguishable and rain water dripped from their noses. Thunder growled closer to them now and the wind picked up slightly. Ahead some two hundred yards lay the now-sleeping camp of Charlie Roundtree and his renegades. By a light touch on the shoulder, Eli signaled his companions to separate and move off at predetermined angles to search for sentries. Eli continued straight ahead.

He saw the sleepy guard two minutes later, in the glare of a distant lightning flash. The clouds hung low, the blackness of a tremendous thunderstorm blotting out the entire south and west. The scout knew his crouching approach would probably go unnoticed. From the slight build of the lookout, Holten figured him to be one of the young men who had watched the village when he had escaped. Charlie had probably put him on the two-to-four guard mount as punishment. Cautiously, his feet clad in Sioux moccasins, Holten slipped up on the unsuspecting man.

When he reached a point close enough to strike, Eli drew his Bowie and held it low, edge up. His target turned away and the scout stepped in closer.

He could smell the odor of meat cooked over an open fire. Apparently the young renegade had brought along something to snack on. Holten wished him good appetite as he covered the final distance and clamped a hand over the half-breed's mouth.

At the same time, he swung the Bowie around in a wide arc. The blade sunk deeply into the victim's abdomen, angled upward to pierce the diaphragm. It went in with only slight difficulty and Holten held the quavering youth until his death throes ended. Eli removed his knife and eased the corpse to the ground. Immediately he moved on, at an oblique angle, seeking the next sentry.

Horses nickered and the aroma of their droppings rose in the damp night air. The rain was getting heavier and the beasts had become restless because the pungent odor of ozone warned of rapidly approaching thunderheads. Arkady Twopots reached out a hand and rubbed the soft nose of the nearest stallion. He liked horses, got along well with them. He had even obtained a job in a livery stable, where he had been content with the money he'd earned and the chance to be close to his favorite animals. Then Charlie Roundtree had come along with his talk of driving out the whites.

If Warren Colfax hadn't come into town and gotten drunk and beaten hell out of that "stinkin' breed," as he had called Arkady, perhaps the young quarter-breed would never have joined up with the renegade army. It had seemed, at the time, a good way to get even. And he had.

When they'd raided the small ranch where Warren Colfax worked as a hand, Arkady had personally held down the bullying cowboy and slit his throat. After that, he had no choice but to remain with the raiders, in the hope that Charlie's scheme might succeed. Now he had rather large doubts about that possibility.

The Army had come into the fight. Charlie had promised that they would not, could not, by law. Instead of a sheriff's posse of bumbling farmers and lazy, town loafers, they faced trained soldiers. Worse, the blue-legs had the awful long knives with them. Those pointed, spikelike devices terrified Arkady. He had seen his best friend among the renegade band stabbed with one in Haggard. Ponca Bill had screamed and wriggled on the deady steel until the soldier who'd stuck it in him fired a shot that had blown Bill's belly apart and had released the blood-dripping metal shaft. Remembering, Arkady shuddered. He hoped he would never be cut with anything like that.

A moment later, Eli Holten destroyed Arkady's aspirations.

Cold steel broke a fiery trail through Arkady's back as Holten held a hand over his mouth. The Bowie struck twice on each side of his spine, destroying both kidneys. Arkady Twopots stiffened, then went limp, unable to make the slightest sound. With practiced ease, the scout put the empty husk aside and moved over to the corral.

Lifting the poles so they made no betraying sound, Holten eased out all but the top rail of the gate. That would come later, when the shooting started. By now, he estimated, the mounted men, under Sergeant O'Kelly, would be in position to charge. So far, thanks to his skill and the gathering storm, the camp dogs had not even sounded an alarm. Holten cleaned his blade and drifted off toward the low lodges.

He and his four men moved closer until they could see the prone forms of the sleeping rene- gades through the flaps of the tipis and brush huts. Some stirred and muttered as thunder growled and the world turned stark white in the brief blaze of a lightning bolt. Eli Holten lowered himself to all fours and slid along the ground, his com- panions following suit. Each headed directly for the lodge where he would find his target. Holten wanted to make sure they got in close enough for one-shot kills. Mostly he wanted Roundtree out of the picture.

In Charlie's buffalo-hide tipi, a saddle that Holten recognized as Charlie's acted as a pillow for a snoring form. The scout eased his Remington out and held it close to his body. A sudden, chill squall, that raced ahead of the coming tumult, rattled the leaves of the cottonwoods. Holten used that sound to cover the cocking of his revolver. Ready now, he inched close to the sleeping man in the lodge. With the .44's muzzle only a foot away from the renegade's skull, Eli pulled the trigger.

Muzzle bloom and a ferocious roar blotted out the heavenly pyrotechnics for an instant. Im- mediately following his shot, Holten heard four more in rapid succession. From the distance,

233

O'Kelly's voice reached him.

"Chee-aaar-rrrge!"

A new thunder filled the sheltered bend as hoofbeats pounded on the sand.

Across the lodge, two man-forms away from the mixed-blood whose skull Holten had just splattered over the hide walls, another renegade leaped up just as an awesome blaze of lightning struck the opposite bank. In the glare, Holten recognized Roundtree.

"Charlie!" he bellowed, his voice lost in an incredible peal of thunder.

Charlie had seen the scout and turned his way. He fired wildly and dived under the rolled-up skirt of the tipi. Holten's return bullet cracked harmlessly through the tipi cover above Charlie's head. By then pandemonium had broken loose outside.

Soldiers and civilians opened up with volleys of deadly fire, cutting into the staggering, befuddled renegades. Charlie's dark form darted in among his followers. Holten pounded after him, slipping on a slick patch of mud exposed by the rains. Then Charlie located his drunken, white renegade bugler.

"Sound 'To Arms' damn it, 'To Arms'! Blow 'Assembly' . . . no, 'Echelon Right.' Get over there," he screamed at some confused breeds. "They're coming from the right. Fire, you sons of bitches, *fire!*"

A bullet from Holten's six-gun cracked past Charlie's head and he ducked low. In a moment he had disappeared from the scout's sight.

Notes squawked from the tarnished bugle, blurry, due to a soft lip caused by sucking too long on a whiskey bottle.

234

From above on the bluff, a big buffalo rifle cracked. The bugler staggered backward a step before he threw his instrument to the sky and fell into the glowing embers of a banked cookfire. Flames crackled from several lodges now, casting a ghastly yellow light on the combatants. They and the corpse of the bugler continued to sizzle though sheets of heavy raindrops lashed down out of the rumbling, pitch-dark clouds. Instinctively, Holten headed toward the pole corral.

Charlie Roundtree had beaten him there.

Holten had to work his way through the squirming, grappling knots of whites and renegades who battled with a ferocity born in hell. He leaped over a renegade and a soldier who rolled on the ground, knives in their hands. The danger he exposed himself to came home to Eli when a round from the bluffs creased the top of his shoulder.

Although painful and numbing, it had not broken the skin, the scout noted as he pounded up to where Charlie worked frantically to throw a saddle on a skitterish horse. At the sound of Holten's approach, Charlie dropped the leather and leaped at the scout.

Muscular bodies crashed together and recoiled slightly. Roundtree had gotten inside Holten's gunhand and fired his own revolver at point-blank range. The hammer fell on an empty chamber. Surprised, Charlie leaped backward. Involuntarily, Holten squeezed his own trigger.

The muzzle hovered under Charlie's armpit when Eli's revolver went off. The renegade howled in agony at the searing flame and hot gases as prickly bits of unburnt powder speckled his flesh. Reflex action closed his arm and he jerked the Remington from Holten's grasp.

Each man had a knife and each knew how to use it well. Holten's Bowie glittered wickedly in the rapid-fire blazes of lightning as he advanced on his enemy. Charlie pulled a long, slim-bladed Green River and slashed viciously at the menacing scout. But before a telling blow could be struck by the half breed or Holten, a rifle butt smashed into the back of the scout's head.

He went down, face first, into the wet sand.

"They got us hemmed in, Charlie. We gotta get out of here fast!" Joe Sureshot shouted.

"Let me finish that one first," Charlie growled, advancing on Holten's prone body.

"Not time. Get a horse now or the damned Army will be havin' yer liver for breakfast."

Three more of Charlie's followers appeared out of the tumult of battle. They confirmed this prediction. All five men slipped hackamores on the few remaining horses and mounted them bareback. They leaped their animals over the low corral rail at the back of the camp and started off at a wild gallop.

Groaning, Holten came to his knees in time to see Charlie and his henchmen racing toward the narrow bank at the western end of camp. Rifles cracked there and one of the fleeing renegades somersaulted over the rump of his galloping steed. In a flash, the remaining quartet ran through their attackers without suffering further loss. Still unsteady, Holten got to his feet and started back across the campsite.

Eli made his way through the withering fire of the whites, rebounding off grappling men, in search of his horse. Twice he fended off the attacks of wild-eyed renegades running from the howling mass of palefaces who had descended on their sanctuary. Into the dark outer limits the scout labored until he came to the tree where he had tied Sonny. Groaning at the throbbing in his head, he swung into the saddle and made off in pursuit of Charlie Roundtree and his three men.

Already the Army had begun to mop up. All resistance had broken and it became only a matter of cornering and disarming the mixed-bloods and their women. The enraged civilians shouted encouragement as they began to fashion hangman's knots from rope they'd found nearby.

"No need to take 'em back," Joshuah Powers shouted to the grinning soldiers as they rounded up yet more of the murderous renegades. "We'll save everybody a lot of time and money. Hang 'em here!"

Chapter Twenty

Eli rode into the night, ahead of the gathering storm. By the lingering glow of lightning flashes he read the fleeing renegades' trail as if it were a message left expressly for him. The convenient sign made him wary. He could be riding into a trap. The sky exploded with brightness again and he saw the fleeing renegades on a slope ahead. He drew his Winchester and reined Sonny in.

Holten raised his weapon to his shoulder and waited. A few seconds passed and a brilliant thunderbolt once more illuminated the rolling ground. In its brief glare, Holten triggered a round.

One rider tumbled from his mount, arms and legs flung wide. His companions paused in their flight for only a moment, then kicked their horses back to a gallop. Alert for any possibility, Holten rode up to the fallen man.

Feebly the renegade tried to aim a revolver at the scout. Holten finished him with another .44-40 slug from the Winchester. At the top of the rise, Holten saw his quarry again in a momentary white glare. He had their bearings now. They were headed for Dodge City.

And why not? Holten considered. Half-breeds had been walking the streets with impunity for years. Through their contacts, they should be able to slither through the slimier cracks of the tough frontier town with ease. Eli returned the Winchester to its saddle scabbard and gave Sonny his head.

An unrestrained tempest swept over the prairie. Caught in its path, Eli Holten was forced to slow his horse as blinding rain and pelting hail descended upon him. Any sane man would have sought shelter. The scout knew he dare not. He estimated the renegade leaders had only a quarter-mile lead. He had to keep going in order to run them to ground in Dodge. Unable to see much beyond Sonny's ears, Holten pressed his relentless pursuit.

Joe Sureshot jumped on Eli first.

Only a split second behind him came Coohooty Smith. They piled into the scout and clung tightly to him, dragging Holten off his horse.

The trio rolled on the sodden, muddy ground. Holten managed to kick Smith in the crotch and momentarily put him out of the fight. Then pain exploded in Eli's head as Joe Sureshot landed a powerful punch above the scout's left ear. With tremendous effort, Holten broke free and came up, vision swimming, to face two knives.

Fearful of attracting more searching soldiers, the two mixed-bloods refrained from using their own firearms. Eli took a step backward, away from the menacing blades. It put him among the snorting horses. He reached for his Bowie. His disappearance drew Coohooty Smith incautiously after him.

Raw steel glowed an unearthly blue in the next heavenly flash. Metal rang on metal as knives clashed together. Smith tried a short left punch that scraped along Holten's jaw. The scout spun to his right and kicked the half-breed in the side of one knee.

Bone snapped and Smith went down with a howl of anguish. "Git him! Goddammit, git him, Joe!" the injured man wailed.

Holten stepped in and plunged the Bowie to the hilt in Coohooty Smith's abdomen. With all of his force, the scout ripped upward. Blood gushed over Eli's hand and arm. Smith's guts spilled out in smoking, purple-gray coils that pulsed and heaved on the ground as though imbued with life of their own. With each wave of their serpentine motion, the renegade grew weaker. He gazed up appealingly, his mouth working but no sound coming. The scout stared back coldly and expressionlessly.

"Where is he, Coohooty?" Joe called from beyond the restless mounts.

"Right here," Holten told him as he stepped into the open.

Without taking time to appraise his opponent, Joe Sureshot leaped at the scout, his long, slim blade leading the way.

Holten had exchanged the Bowie for the Remington. His first bullet caught Joe in midair.

Sureshot seemed to hang suspended above the ground for a long heartbeat; then he came crashing down. Although seriously wounded, Joe nevertheless was determined to finish the scout as he had been ordered. He rose unsteadily to his feet and brought back an arm to throw his knife over the short distance that separated him from Holten.

With a single twist, the blade sped toward its target.

Only Eli Holten didn't wait around for it to arrive. He sidestepped and fired again. The two-hundred-five-grain bullet took Joe Sureshot an inch below his navel.

Intense, paralyzing pain spread outward through Joe's body. His knees buckled and he went down. Desperate now, no thought to other pursuers, he clawed at the Colt in his holster. It came free as though in slow motion.

How heavy it seemed, he thought, mystified, as he tried to bring it in line with the scout. He saw Holten's weapon come level again, watched the muzzle flash and an initial spurt of smoke. Then everything went black as a slug burned into his forehead and destroyed a large portion of his frontal lobe.

Holten stood over the body a second. That left

only Charlie Roundtree, he thought with satisfaction.

Quickly he mounted Sonny and, oblivious to the torment of half-inch-diameter hail, headed again for Dodge City.

Gasping, aching from the storm's punishment, Charlie Roundtree arrived in Dodge City well ahead of the scout. Hailstones the size of silver dollars cracked boards, punched through roofs, and shattered windows in the dreary-looking town. Charlie's horse slogged through nearly knee-deep mud along the main street. A few lights showed in stores and saloons.

Charlie desperately wanted a little whiskey to banish the chill that wracked his body and food to stave off the ache of hunger that pinched his belly. He couldn't stop now, though. He had to make it to the man who had aided him in his goal of evicting the whites. He had to make it to the captain. That was how Charlie always thought of his friend and partner in crime, no matter his present position.

Charlie had served as a scout with the cavalry regiment to which the captain had belonged. That had been back during the War Between the States. Charlie had liked his years in the Army. He and the captain had gotten along well. They shared similar views on the imbecility of those higher up in command and on the laziness of subordinate troops. They also preferred mules to horses for most purposes. Charlie had served faithfully and well. He'd learned a great deal about command, discipline, and tactics from the captain. Then, after the war, Charlie had gone about his own affairs, having been discharged in the general turnout following the onset of peace.

To his great surprise, after a few years had passed, he'd encountered the captain once again. They'd talked and, out of several days of discussion, had come up with the idea of making a fortune on land speculation. Only not in the usual way. They hadn't the funds to invest heavily in a railroad and thus reap millions of acres for sale or use. So they'd decided to create conditions which would compel people to sell the land they held at unbelievably low prices. Through such distress sales, Charlie and the captain would become rich in land and later in dollars. Charlie glanced furtively around the abandoned streets of Dodge and hoped strongly that the captain was in town, as his last note had said he would be. Then he edged to the side of the avenue and turned into the alleyway he sought.

The half-breed halted his horse before a door and dismounted. He knocked stoutly. Long seconds went by and Charlie knocked again.

Yellowed light from a coal-oil lamp appeared around the cracks at the edge of the door. It grew brighter while Charlie dripped rain and tried to shield his head from the hailstones. He heard the rattle of a key in the lock; then the door was flung wide.

"I'm glad you are here, Captain," Charlie declared as he pushed forward, toward the warmth and dryness inside. "The soldiers got in it, even though you said they couldn't. They hit our camp some hours ago. I'm on the run."

"Come in out of the rain, then," the captain replied. "I can hide you here for a while."

"No good. I want my share of the money so I can go away and wait for things to cool off."

"But . . . that's not possible. I haven't bought up all of the land as yet and no one is buying except our competition."

"Bankers are buying?"

"Yes, at two cents to a nickle on the dollar. We have to wait."

"I cannot wait. I must take my money and hide."

"But I have no money. It is all tied up. Get out of here, Charlie, and wait somewhere else. I'll contact you."

Eli Holten reached Dodge City during a lull in the storm. Powerful winds still lashed the few trees and caused less stout buildings to groan and creak. Rain fell occasionally in swift, drenching showers. To the southwest, more thunderheads threatened. The scout approached warily. He carefully studied the vacant streets and the occasional glow of a lamp from within a shop or house. The more cautious citizens had taken to their storm cellars, he surmised. Halfway down the empty main street, Holten saw a dark silhouette of a man leading a horse.

The animal's head hung down, a sign of

244

extreme fatigue. Water dripped from its shaggy mane. A bolt of exhilaration charged Eli with alertness. He had found his man. Quickly he moved out of sight at the corner of a building. Then the waiting began.

Charlie Roundtree entered a saloon, noisily forcing his way through the closed, rain-warped doors behind the batwings. Silence followed. Holten left Sonny in the shelter of a lean-to behind a boardinghouse and crossed the street to a better vantage point. A sudden drop in temperature told him that the next storm wave was poised close at hand, ready to rampage through the town. Shadows cast by lamplight on the big front windows of the saloon revealed to Eli that only two other customers occupied the barroom with Charlie Roundtree. Still Holten waited.

Like a seething, malicious whisper, rain and hail swept across the rooftops of Dodge City. Charlie had not left the saloon. Holten replaced the cartridges in his Remington with somewhat drier rounds from his belt loops and started across the muddy impasse that had been a street. He held his weapon ready, hammer back and finger hovering outside the trigger guard. When he reached the plankwalk, his sodden moccasins squished softly.

The storm effectively hid any sounds of his approach. As a result, it shocked the inhabitants of the saloon into surprised immobility when he kicked open the twin doors and stood menacingly in the opening.

"Holten!" Charlie Roundtree barked. His hand

clawed for the Colt at his waist.

Eli fired first.

The bullet seared a hot track along the left side of Charlie's rib cage. He groaned and staggered to the left, but kept his feet. He fired, shattering one of the painted glass panels of the front entrance. The close call caused the scout to duck sideways. In the same instant, a brilliant flash of lightning momentarily blinded everyone.

When the scout blinked his eyes into focus again, Charlie had gone. A man lay on the sawdust-covered floor, hands to his head, moaning and writhing feebly. Beyond the stretch of polished mahogany, a flimsy door to the side entrance flapped in the howling maelstrom that assaulted Dodge City. Holten hurried in that direction.

"He went out the side, Eli," the bartender confirmed. Then, almost as an afterthought, he added. "What do you want ol' Charlie for?"

"He's the leader of the renegades," the scout snapped back.

"Oh! I'll get my shotgun and come with you."

"No. I can handle him alone."

"Then I'll get a rope for you after you catch him."

"Good idea." With that, Holten stepped out through the doorway.

A fraction of a second later, a bullet gouged splinters from the clapboard side of the saloon, an inch from Eli's head. He felt a warm trickle of blood from cuts caused by flying shards of wood. Instinctively he fired toward the muzzle blast.

246

It netted him nothing, beyond the squelching sound of retreating footsteps. Determined to end this quickly, the scout pounded down a narrow space between buildings, after Charlie Roundtree. At the rear of the structures, another shot cracked past his head from the cover of an outhouse. He answered with two closely spaced rounds that tore the upper hinge off the chicksale door. Once more he listened to receding steps.

"Charlie! Give yourself up!" Holten cried. He considered this a useless effort, but he had to try.

As expected, he didn't receive an answer.

Large footprints, distorted in the fresh mud, showed Holten the way. Cautiously he entered an intersecting alley. Crouched low, he darted to a spot behind an overflowing rain barrel and hazarded a peek over the top.

Far down the way, Charlie pounded on a door. As the scout watched, a patch of yellow light showed briefly and the renegade dashed inside. Then darkness and rain returned. Swiftly, Holten advanced on the entrance of the building Charlie had entered.

When he reached the doorway, he had no difficulty identifying the place. Strangely, that did not surprise him. He reached out and tried the knob. Bolted, naturally. A heavy slug from the Remington shattered the cast-iron lock case behind the wood panel and the portal swung wide. Warily, Eli stepped inside.

He paused to test the silence and let his eyes adjust to the faint light that came from the second floor. Holten saw muddy footprints on the treads of a narrow staircase and strode in that direction. With practiced care, Eli tested each step to avoid betraying squeaks, slowly ascending toward the beckoning glow. When Holten reached the top, he bent low and again, watched, and listened.

No sounds came to indicate where Charlie and his accomplice might be lurking. The scout eased himself upward enough to complete his climb and then stepped into a pool of shadow in the narrow corridor that ran the width of the back of the building. From an open doorway, lamplight spilled onto the floor of the hall.

One hand extended, Holten eased himself along the rear wall until he came to the illuminated opening. Once more he ducked low and entered with a rush, the muzzle of his Remington leading the way.

The sight that greeted Holten jolted him to an abrupt stop. Eyes suddenly widened, mouth partly open, Eli stared at the bound and abused body of lovely Susan Walters. Blood ran from cuts and weals on her thighs and chest, and ugly burns disfigured both her breasts. Horror-fed rage raced through the scout's sturdy frame. Driven to fury, he turned about to seek the ones responsible for this outrage.

Faster than an eyeblink, an object flashed by his face. The iron rod struck his forearm, an inch above his wrist, and his Remington fell from inoperative fingers. Before Holten could move, Charlie Roundtree stepped into his line of vision, a cocked Colt pointed at the scout's chest. Holten heard movement to his left.

A naked, gloating Hiram Skaggs stepped into view. It had been he who'd wielded the rod that had disarmed Holten.

"Well, you came at an opportune time, Holten," Skaggs purred in oily satisfaction. "Now I can kill both of you and no one will ever know of my involvement in this." He stepped closer, savoring his ultimate victory.

"You'll go first, scout. That way your slut there will lose all hope and finally become frantic at the realization of her own fate. It will make the pleasure of killing her a great deal more intense."

"You've been behind this all the time?" Holten inquired, still uncertain of the details.

"Of course, my boy. You didn't think those whiskey-rotted half-breeds had sense enough to create such a grand design, did you?"

"How did you come up with this mad scheme?" the scout asked, trying to keep his voice calm. He knew he had to buy all the time he could. Holten combed through his scattered thoughts and memories. He had to keep Skaggs talking, had to hope for some distraction that would allow him to act.

"Mad is it? Hardly that. You see, I have hated the Army for a long time. I knew they must be disgraced and humbled for what they did to me?"

"What was that?"

"Long ago, they drummed me out of the service. Stripped me of rank and flogged me and made a public spectacle of my humiliation. For that they had to pay!" A ring of hysteria tinged the obese banker's words. "It took a while to come upon the right circumstances. But here, in Dodge City, I found them ready and waiting. With an incompetent like Lemuel Waterstratt in command at Fort Dodge, all of the elements came into place. It was Waterstratt, you see, who cut the epaulettes and buttons from my tunic. He was a captain, like myself, only on the staff. He had never had to face the Confederate artillery or that hideous Rebel yell. Now he was in a place of vulnerability. I could make fools of them all.

"And I have!" Skaggs shouted gleefully. "The Army has failed! The people are leaving in droves and selling their land to me at insultingly low prices. The Army will never find out what happened until I am safely far away and disgustingly wealthy."

"The Army has not failed, Skaggs," Holten told him levelly. "Your gang of renegades has been killed off."

A musing expression crossed the round-faced banker's features. "Have they now? Then the Army has done double service in this matter. They have failed to prevent the exodus and they have eliminated the very ones I would have had to deal with later on. Now that I own all but a tiny portion of the land, it is time for the raids to stop. How nice that the Army did that for me."

"*You* own the land?" Charlie Roundtree growled. "What about our deal, Captain? What about the equal share you owe to me?"

From the roof above them came the cacophonous roar of enormous hailstones as the storm broke again. Hiram Skaggs glanced upward before answering Charlie's challenge. He did so in a sneeringly superior manner.

"*Your* share? How do you propose to get it? Why, all of the property purchased is indeed in my name. You haven't a claim to anything. You don't think you can walk into a court and demand it, now do you?"

"Then . . . all I have to show for the risks I took, for the men who died fighting for me, is . . . is your profit?"

"You're learning, Charlie. But you are still a foolish stupid half-breed. I never intended to share anything with you. As a matter of fact," the bloated banker went on as he snatched up Holten's Remington from the table where Charlie had placed it, "I figured to kill you right along with Holten and Susan here.

"You see, you forced your way in here, shot the both of them and I killed you. I will have brought an end to the leader of the evil raiders, and I will even become something of a hero."

An icy smile curled Charlie Roundtree's lips. "It is you who are stupid, Captain. You made the mistake of sending several notes to me, to pass on information about good places to attack. They are all in the same handwriting and you even signed three of them. I saved those notes."

Hiram Skaggs's face blanched. He worked his mouth, but no words came.

"Did you think you would be the first white

251

man to cheat me?" Charlie thundered over the bellow of the storm. "I took precautions of my own. That's right, I saved those notes. They're in a safety deposit box right here in your bank. I used a false name, of course, and I had Randy Talmadge, my bugler open the account and bring them in. My copy of the key is in a safe place, too. How would it look if your words were revealed to the Army? If I don't come out of here safe and alive, they will be. And, for that matter, I expect to come away from here with two-thirds of the land titles deeded over to me, not half like you promised."

Skaggs had gone gray, yet fires leaped behind the clear lenses of his eyes. He breathed in gasps, as though physically assaulted by every one of Charlie's words. At last he could give voice to his rage.

"That's blackmail!" he shrieked. Made unmindful of Charlie's threat by his fury, Skaggs swung the muzzle of Holten's Remington toward the renegade.

Charlie shot Skaggs in the thigh.

The banker gave out a yowl of pain and staggered backward. In that calamitous instant, the scout saw his chance.

Abandoning caution, Holten leaped between the two men and grabbed the Remington from Skaggs's limp fingers. To ensure that he captured the weapon, he drove a hard left into the pudgy banker's chest.

The blow sent Skaggs stumbling through the room.

Too far, Hiram Skaggs discovered as he crashed through the window and fell, screaming in terror, to the muddy street below. Propelled by the same movement, Eli Holten continued his turn until he saw the surprised face of Charlie Roundtree. Quickly, Eli cocked the Remington and lined the muzzle on the center of Charlie's chest.

A second horrendous blast raised plaster dust from the walls and set the cobwebs to swaying. The .44-40 bullet crossed the short space and slammed into Charlie's sternum.

Gamely, the half-breed tried to ear back the hammer of his Colt and return fire. Eli didn't give him time enough.

The final round in the Remington made a popping sound as it punched out Charlie Roundtree's front teeth and angled upward through the roof of his mouth. Blood squirted from his ears, nose, and eyes, and his obsidian orbs bulged outward from hydrostatic shock as hot lead destroyed his otherwise fine mind.

As the body fell, Holten stepped to the desk and cut Susan free. She moaned at the pain that needled through every inch of her flesh and swallowed to remove the taste of the gag which had been replaced at the sound of Holten's forced entrance to the building. Instead of a jamble of words of gratitude, Susan made a grim request as she tugged free of Holten's gingerly embrace.

"I . . . want to see."

With that, she crossed to the window, one hand holding on to Holten's soggy buckskin shirt sleeve so that he trailed after her. They gazed down, into the darkened street.

The fall had broken both of Hiram Skaggs's legs. He writhed weakly in the mud, while fist-sized hail pounded his body to a bloody pulp. Eli and Susan watched for a long while as nature's ice bullets pummeled the banker to death.

THE NEWEST ADVENTURES AND ESCAPADES OF BOLT
by Cort Martin

#10: BAWDY HOUSE SHOWDOWN   (1176, $2.25)
The best man to run the new brothel in San Francisco is Bolt. But Bolt's intimate interviews lead to a shoot-out that has the city quaking—and the girls shaking!

#11: THE LAST BORDELLO   (1224, $2.25)
A working girl in Angel's camp doesn't stand a chance—unless Jared Bolt takes up arms to bring a little peace to the town . . . and discovers that the trouble is caused by a woman who used to do the same!

#12: THE HANGTOWN HARLOTS   (1275, $2.25)
When the miners come to town, the local girls are used to having wild parties, but events are turning ugly . . . and murderous. Jared Bolt knows the trade of tricking better than anyone, though, and is always the first to come to a lady in need . . .

#13: MONTANA MISTRESS   (1316, $2.25)
Roland Cameron owns the local bank, the sheriff, and the town— and he thinks he owns the sensuous saloon singer, Charity, as well. But the moment Bolt and Charity eye each other there's fire—especially gunfire!

#14: VIRGINIA CITY VIRGIN   (1360, $2.25)
When Katie's bawdy house holds a high stakes raffle, Bolt figures to take a chance. It's winner take all—and the prize is a budding nineteen year old virgin! But there's a passle of gun-toting folks who'd rather see Bol in a coffin than in the virgin's bed!

#15: BORDELLO BACKSHOOTER   (1411, $2.25)
Nobody has ever seen the face of curvaceous Cherry Bonner, the mysterious madam of the bawdiest bordello in Cheyenne. When Bolt keeps a pimp with big ideas and a terrible temper from having his way with Cherry, gunfire flares and a gambling man would bet on murder: Bolt's!

MORE OF THE HOTTEST WESTERNS!

GUNN #18: THE GOLDEN LADY   (1298, $2.25)
by Jory Sherman
Gunn's got a beautiful miner's daughter in front of him, and hard-case killers closing in on him from the rear. It looks like he'll be shooting in all directions!

GUNN #19: HIGH MOUNTAIN HUSSY   (1348, $2.25)
by Jory Sherman
Gunn gets intimate with a dark-haired temptress—and she's revealing it all! Her father's been murdered, but not before writing a cryptic message that Gunn's obliged to decipher—before a killer deciphers Gunn!

GUNN #20: TEN-GALLON TEASE   (1378, $2.25)
by Jory Sherman
With Apache raiders and a desperate outlaw gang each planning an ambush, Gunn's chance to make fast money selling California horses to the U.S. Cavalry looks slim. He's lucky he can count on the services of a wild and beautiful tomboy to help him in the clinches!

SHELTER #18: TABOO TERRITORY   (1379, $2.25)
by Paul Ledd
A ruthless death-battalion member is Shelter's target—but Shelter's got to get the Baja to take his shot. And with the help of a dark-haired Baja beauty, he may just succeed!

SHELTER #19: THE HARD MEN   (1428, $2.25)
by Paul Ledd
Shelter's aiming to cross another member of the death battalion off his hit list—except he's hunting the wrong man. Morgan's in for trouble, and it takes the hot touch of an eager squaw to get him ready for action!

SHELTER #20: SADDLE TRAMP   (1464, $2.25)
by Paul Ledd
Tracking another killer, Shelter takes on the identity of a murdered U.S. marshal and lays down the law. And a buxom bargirl named Lola likes the way the law lays!

Available wherever paperbacks are sold, or order direct from the Publisher. Send cover price plus 50¢ per copy for mailing and handling to Zebra Books, 475 Park Avenue South, New York, N.Y. 10016. DO NOT SEND CASH.